MW01231763

Perfect love casts out all fear

1 John 4:18

Be Captured

Brenda

ANGEL WING MINISTRIES PRESENTS

...

PERFECT LOVE

CARRIED BY ANGELS SERIES

BOOK NUMBER 2

Brenda Conley
Angel Wing Ministries

COVER DESIGN
CREATED
BY

BRANDON ANDRINA

COVER PHOTOS
BY

SARA COMBS
PHOTOGRAPHY

AND

LISA RENEE
PHOTOGRAPHY

Library of Congress Cataloging in-Publication Data
Conley, Brenda
Perfect Love/Brenda Conley
ISBN-13: 978-0615891774 (Angel Wing Ministries)
ISBN-10: 0615891772

DEDICATION

This book belongs to all the broken women who live everyday with the grief of losing a child to the lies of abortion.

God sees your brokenness. He wants to restore you. Our God is in the restoration business and He loves you.

Do not let satan tell you differently. He wants you to live a lifetime of brokenness. He is a liar who comes to kill, steal and destroy. He will never have a victory unless you give it to him. He has already been defeated. Jesus himself went into hell and took back the keys so that satan could have no control over any area of your life.

There is no sin that is too big for our God to forgive. He does not want you to live a life carrying a load of regret. He made a way through His Son Jesus Christ to lighten that load and give you hope. In fact, He will pick you up and carry you when the road seems to long… when you are too weary…when you have gone as far as you can…when you can see no hope at the end of the day..

If you are still burdened with choices that you made, today is the day to lay them at the feet of Jesus. He is just waiting for you to come just as you are. Broken and spilled out, surrendered to Him. Feel the freedom that only He can give. Run to His mercy seat and live with joy. Jesus is just waiting to change your life. He wants to give you a life everlasting full of love, hope and peace; the peace that surpasses all understanding.

By ourselves we will never be worthy. But through Christ all things are possible. He loves you enough that He laid down His life for you so that you could live a life abundant. You were created with a purpose. God knew that purpose even before you were brought into this world. Seek Him. Find Him. Live for Him.

PSALM 18:30-32
As for God, His way is perfect;
The word of the LORD is flawless.
He is a shield
For all who take refuge in Him.
For who is God besides the LORD?
And who is the Rock except our God?
It is God who arms me with strength
And makes my way perfect.

1 JOHN 4: 15-18
If anyone acknowledges that Jesus is the Son of God,
God lives in him and he in God.
And so we know and rely on the love God has for us.
God is love.
Whoever lives in love lives in God, and God in him.
In this way love is made complete among us so that we
will have confidence on the day of judgment,
Because in this world we are like Him.
There is no fear in love.
But perfect love drives out fear,
Because fear has to do with punishment.
The one who fears is not made perfect in love.

Those of you who began this journey with Noelle in the first book, SAVING NOELLE, know that the second book was to be LOVE ABOUNDS.

These books have always been a direction of God. However, as we began the editing process, again He took us in a different direction. Why should we be surprised? He loves to keep us on our toes waiting for His next move. Love His sense of humor.

Isaiah 55:8
"For my thoughts are not your thoughts,
Neither are your ways my ways,"
declares the Lord

As the characters of this journey continue on, the theme of the second book begins to show the perfect love of God. We walk through their struggles and see God's face as He pursues with an unfailing love. Our God is relentless and yes…He is perfect.

The amazing part of God is that He willingly enters our lives daily and He speaks to us when life is very normal. Look at Abram when God spoke to him for the first time. It was described in a devotional bible like this, "There was no roar of thunder, Abram wasn't suddenly surrounded by a mysterious darkness, he wasn't transported to a dimension transcending time, space or usual definition. The Scriptures just say that God spoke."

That is how He speaks to us also. Too many times, we miss his voice in the noise of our day, loud music, TV blaring, the clatter of the world surrounding us.

Brad and Noelle were listening and through the time that they spent in conversation with their Heavenly Father, He directed them into a love for each other and bound them by the love of Christ. They built their foundation on the Rock. They made a choice that they would wake up every day and choose to love not through their own strength but by the power of Christ's perfect love. See where that commitment takes them in this second book in the CARRIED BY ANGELS SERIES, now titled, PERFECT LOVE.

ACKNOWLEDGEMENTS

Praise God from whom all blessings flow. Without Him, I could not do any of this. It was His idea, His message and His provision that allowed me to write these words. He is my Lord and Savior, The Keeper of my heart, My Provider, My Deliverer, My One and Only, My All in All. I love You Lord. Use me as a vessel to carry your story around the world.

Thank you to all of the brave women who were willing to share their experiences with me. Without all of you these books would not have been written. I am so proud of each one of you. Because of you, God allowed me to write His message of hope. God began to drop each of you into my life and you opened your hearts and shared your pain and suffering. If through these words, one woman makes the decision to choose life for her baby, then heaven will rejoice. God bless all of you as you walk towards a forgiving Father whose arms stretch out wide. My prayer is that God will use these books to reach multitudes of people who believe there is only one way. I pray these books will be a vessel for the broken that cannot see past their sorrow, a way to conquer the fear that they may find themselves living with everyday. Let God have His way in your life. Feel His love. My hope is to strengthen young women before…

To Ron. My best friend. My husband for 39 years. You have been there through it all. Your strength continues to amaze me. You walked along my side through the good and the bad. You have been there for the happy and the sad. We have laughed and cried. I pray that God will continued to bring us closer to Him as we walk together towards eternity. We are learning everyday to trust where He is taking us. I would not want to walk this path with anyone else. Thank you for loving me.

To my children from birth and marriage. You make me laugh and you make me cry. I could not be prouder of who you are becoming. Seek first His Kingdom and all things will He add unto you. You are a mighty force. God has a plan. Never step out from under His protective umbrella. You are the righteousness of God in Christ. God chooses you; you are blessed and you are loved.

To my grandchildren. You make me young. I love watching you grow. You are eager and excited. Life holds such adventure for you. Your Poppi and Gammy pray that God will pour His favor on each of you. May you always see the majesty of who He is and may your life reflect the glory of God. God chooses you; you are blessed and you are loved.

To you my family, I speak into your life the promises of God. You are growing into righteous people of God. You will stand in the evil day having your loins girded about with truth; you will have the breastplate of righteousness. Your feet will be shod with the gospel of peace. You take up the shield of faith. You are covered with the helmet of salvation, and you will use the sword of the Spirit, which is the Word of God. God chooses you; you are blessed and you are loved.

To all of you…God is why I write. Without His lead, there would be no words. It has been my pleasure to bring you His messages of hope. Do not take my word for it though. Pick up a Bible. Find a lifetime full of love and wisdom. See how much He really loves you. Nothing can compare to the real deal. He is waiting for you in the pages of His word. He has a special message, created just for you that only He can deliver. He is that personal. Let Him love you.

TO GOD BE THE GLORY, GREAT THINGS HE HAS DONE

All My Love,

Mom

STORY CHARACTERS

Naming the characters in my stories is like giving birth to my own children. I have always thought it important that they have strong names that will serve them well through life. I decided it was important that I share with you why I chose the names of the people that you would meet in this story.

Noelle--(French origin meaning "born at Christmas time) she is a broken 19 year old. The oldest daughter in what was supposed to be a wonderful family. If asked, they would tell you that they are Christians; however, Christmas, Easter and marriages sum up their church life experience as a family. Noelle and her sisters attended summer Vacation Bible School programs and you will see how the Word of God is faithful. You will walk with her through a life changing experience. See how God made a way for her through all of it. All she had to do was look at His hand guiding and directing her path.

Brad Conroy--(English origin meaning "one who has broad shoulders") a hard working 22 year old whose life is about to change as he follows his heart into an area of God's leading. Brad is faithful to wait upon the Lord and wise enough to honor his father and mother. See the turn his life takes, as he is obedient to the Lord.

Eyan Conroy--(Gaelic origin; form of John meaning "God is gracious") Brad's brother. They are different and yet so close. He loves and respects his brother. At 20 years old, he is ready to embrace the world. Eyan is looking to branch out into the world of the unknown. Living on the farm is not in his future. His passion is to reach the lost for the Lord out on a mission field somewhere adventurous.

Angelina Conroy--(Greek form of Angela, meaning "a heavenly messenger; an angel") her name really represents the part that she will play in Noelle's life. Angelina is a survivor; full of wisdom and willing to walk through the ugliness of her past life to help save the life of an unborn child.
Terran Conroy--(Latin origin; Man of the earth) Angelina's husband, Brad, and Eyan's father. A wonderful man who left this earth too soon. They miss him desperately. He lives on in the character of the boys as they grow into the men he would have wanted them to be.
Genie Smith--(English origin; form of Jean meaning, "God is gracious") Noelle's mother. Trying to heal from a broken marriage, her focus becomes her girls.
Gale Smith--(Irish origin meaning a foreigner) this was the husband to Genie and father to their daughters. His leaving caused a hole in their family that left them trying to figure out who they are. He really did become a foreigner to them.
Debbie--(Hebrew origin; in the Bible a prophetess) Genie's sister. She loves her sister and nieces and wants only to help support them.
Nissa--(Hebrew origin; meaning "one who tests others") the middle sister. Thrust into becoming the protector in the home. She loves her sisters desperately and is the peacemaker in the family. Seventeen years old and starting her senior year of high school.
Anaya--(African origin; meaning "One who looks up to God) the youngest of the three girls. Anaya and Noelle have the closest bond of the girls. She feels Noelle's pain the most. She is going to be sixteen.
Michael Dunn--(Hebrew origin; meaning, "Who is like God") Genie's boss. His life is touched by watching this family walk through fire and come out on the other side with a deeper relationship with the Lord.
Michelle Jordan--(French origin and feminine form of

Michael meaning, "Who is like God") She, apart from anyone else, will be able to come along side Noelle. They will become friends through an understanding of brokenness. **Shawn**--(Irish origin and a form of John, meaning, "God is gracious") Shawn is laughter when times get hard. There is always a smile waiting from him. He is one of the broken that God dropped into the Conroy's lives. His early years were full of sorrow and sadness. **Pastor Travis Gates**--(French meaning, "To cross over") Brad's youth pastor. He has been a grounding point for the Conroy boys while they were growing up. He will be helpful in showing Noelle the way towards healing through Christ. **Rebecca Gates**—(Hebrew meaning, "One who is bound to God") she is Pastor Travis' wife and they exhibit a love joined through Christ. She brings completeness to Travis. **Delmyn Whitehall**--(English origin meaning a man of the mountain) this is a troubled young man. His life was full of money and no responsibility. There has been no accountability until his world comes crashing down around him. This man will represent an amazing opportunity to practice forgiveness. **Tempo (Teo for short) Mohan**--(Spanish meaning a godly man) An attorney who's path will cross Delmyn's and will have an impact on this young man's life.

Come along with me as we follow our friends through this new adventure. Be prepared for the turns that this story will take. They even surprised me. Noelle has so many decisions to make. She has so much to learn. However, praise God that she has put her life in greater hands… The Hands of God…who holds every tear that we cry.

FORWARD

Ecclesiastes 3:1

There is a time for everything, and a season for every activity under heaven

It was a lazy Saturday morning. I was home when my phone rang. There was an attendant from what I assumed to be a nursing home asking me if I could take a call from one of their residents. She had a southern accent, I was not sure from where; but I immediately said yes. There was a long pause while I waited for someone to speak. She did. I could tell that the woman was frail and her hearing was weak; but her determination was strong. We struggled through our conversation which consisted mostly of her talking and me listening. She wanted to tell me a story. I listened intently and with her permission, I will share it with you. This is her story, sweetly told by the woman who did not even tell me her name.

Honey I want to tell you my story. Perhaps it is my time. I am old. No one knows my story. I have lived a long, happy life. My husband has been gone for many years. I am ready to be gone when God calls me.

Years ago, I lived in times that were hard. There had been a depression in the country and families were still struggling to put food on the table. Stress was high and people did crazy things. I was from a large family. We worked the fields and grew a big garden. We ate out of that garden so food for us was not the issue that it was for people in other places. Our family lived in a small shack in the south. The men worked where they could find work. One day I was working in a cotton field. It was starting to get dark. I was so tired. It had been a long day. People were starting to leave, so I did too. I still had a mile walk ahead of me. There was a neighbor man following me who had been working in the field too. He started out a distance behind me; but he was gaining ground and making the space between us less. I heard him call out to me and there was a sickening feeling in my stomach. He was old. I was 15. He was saying things to me that were not nice. I started to run. He caught me and dragged me into the bushes. What happened was ugly and no young girl should have to know.

Afterwards he left me there. It was dark and I was on the ground crying. A long time went by. I was afraid to go home. My mom sent my older sisters to look for me. I heard them call my name and I answered back. They sat on the ground and cried with me.

A couple of months went by and I did not feel very well. I was sick every morning when I woke up. I did not want to think about what was going on. I had seen this happen to my mom many times. After she was sick, there was always a baby. I did not want a baby. I did not want a baby from that man.

I told my sister and she knew a girl who had gone to this woman, who was kind of like a doctor, and the problem went away. She took me to the woman's home.

The woman said she would help me and that she would not tell anyone. It hurt and after a few days, I did not throw up any more.

It seemed harmless at the time, but it was not. All of my life I wondered about that baby. There were always questions in my mind. What happened to the baby that she took out of me? Did that baby know what I did? Will God punish me for it?

I married a nice man and we moved away. We moved to Michigan and we had a nice life. However, I never got to be a mother. It just did not happen. We worked hard and had a comfortable life. I missed not holding a baby. I believed that God was just punishing me because of what I did.

Then one day we went to a church where they were having a revival. We learned that God is a God of love. They told us that if we accepted Jesus Christ as the Savior of our lives, He would forgive our sins. We found out He died on the cross for our sins and that His blood would cleanse us of all wrongdoing. I wanted that and so did my husband. We gave our lives to Jesus that night.

Our lives did not change on the outside. We still went to work everyday and came home to take care of our home. What did change was our hearts. We were happier and we joined that church and had a sense of belonging. We knew God loved us and we had a community of people who loved us too. We worked hard in the church until we became too old to help them much. Then they helped us. They were there to help me when my husband died and they have been there for me now that I am living out the rest of my life.

I never told my husband about the mean man or the lost baby. I told God and He forgave me. I found peace so that I could let the past be in the past.

I want people to know if they have lost a baby, they do not have to let the devil beat them up. They can find God. He is a God of forgiveness and He will heal the sadness inside of them. Otherwise, it could destroy them. I know.

I read the book SAVING NOELLE and I wished that I could have been someone like Angelina who could help someone by telling her story. I do not want to die with my story locked away inside.   Maybe I can help someone if I can tell you this.

Thank you.

She hung up.

This is her story as close to her words as I could retell it. I do not know where the woman was from or how she got my book. I tried to call the number back and it was an unidentified number. I googled the area code from my caller ID and found out it was southwestern Alabama. I am thankful that God brought her to me and that I am able to give her an avenue to tell her story. I pray that her life will be a blessing while she waits for the arms of Jesus to carry her home. Rest my sweet lady. God hears your pleas. Your story is not "just inside of you anymore".

INTRODUCTION

Bless all of you wonderful readers who have followed Noelle from the first book of this series into this chapter of her journey. This book will continue to address the lies of abortion and the brokenness it brings. My desire is to help all of those who live everyday with the sorrow and pain of this horrendous plague on our nation. These books are to be a message of hope. We have a marvelous Savior who loves us more than we can comprehend. He is a forgiving God. His arms are open wide and He is just waiting for you to come and lay down all of the baggage that has been burdening you. He has given you His Word and in it, He says:

"Come to me, all you who are weary and burdened, and I will give You rest. Take my yoke upon you and learn from me, for I am gentle and humble in heart, and you will find rest for your souls. For my yoke is easy and my burden is light. Matthew 11:28-30

You see God never intended that we would carry the sorrows of this world. In fact, His word tells us that in this world we will have troubles. However, our hope is in Him who overcame this world. He wanted us to come to Him and allow Him to carry our burdens and heal our broken hearts. In Him, there is no condemnation. He loves us equally. He loves us enough that He sent Jesus, His son, a man of no sin, to take upon Himself our sins. Then He carried them with Him to the cross where no man could put Him. He willingly crawled onto that cross for every one of us. However, do not miss the best part…Death could not hold Him there. He overcame hell and the grave so we could have life eternal.

This means by accepting Jesus as our Lord and Savior we can spend forever and ever with Him and He will never leave us.

While we were yet sinners, Christ died for us.
Romans 5:8

Can you see what love it took for the Son of God to become a mere man? He gave it all in pain and suffering so we could have love, peace and life eternal.

If you are one of the casualties of abortion and want to surrender the burden you carry, there is no better day than today. Do not waste one more moment. Run into the waiting arms of a Heavenly Father who loves you more than life itself. Confess your sins. Welcome Him into your heart and accept the love that He has to give you. No more do you have to live a life of regret with pain and sorrow attached. He has a plan and a purpose for your life.

For I know the plans I have for you, declares the
Lord, plans to prosper you and not to harm you, plans
to give you hope and a future.
Jeremiah 29:11

He wants you to have hope. My guess is that it was when you felt hopeless that you saw abortion as your only option. God wants to give you hope. He is light. There is a dark side and I can assure you satan, the master of darkness and evil, wants to take away all of your hope. It is when we feel hopeless that we make choices that do not line up with the Word of God. God is hope. He wants nothing but the best for us. However, He gave us free will. He wants us to come to Him on our own. He did not make us puppets that He can manipulate. He created us in His image just one-step lower than the angels. He wants us to walk along beside Him.

God wants to be a companion. He will never leave us or forsake us. He is always there, even when we choose to ignore Him. Today can be your day. If that is where your heart is please take this moment to pray with me.

Father God, I surrender my life to You. I ask that You come into my heart and be my Lord and Savior. I ask you to forgive my sins. I believe that You died on the cross and then You rose from the grave. I acknowledge that only through You can I be worthy; only by Your grace can I be free. I understand that You cast away my sins as far as the east is from the west. I believe that when You look at me, You see me pure, sinless and white as snow. I can rest assured knowing that I will spend eternity with You. Thank You Father for loving me. Amen.

Congratulations. You did it. You just made the most important decision that you will ever make. God loves you. Don't look back. Look forward to your new future. Get your hands on a Bible and begin to read it. Bury His words in your heart. His word is a road map for your life. Your sins are forgiven. Now… get prepared. Satan will come after you. Remember he does not want you living free. Satan thrives on keeping you in bondage. Jesus came so that you might have life and have it more abundantly. Enjoy your freedom.

So if the Son sets you free,
you will be free indeed.
John 8:36

Therefore, if anyone is in Christ,
he is a new creation; the old is gone,
the new has come.
IICorinthians 5:17

HALLELUJAH!

Let the heavens rejoice.

Chapter One

Psalm 96:1

Sing to the Lord

a new song;

Sing to the Lord,

all the earth

NOELLE SAT DOWN AT A BACK TABLE WITH A SALAD and a glass of water. This was her first free moment since the lunch crowd had started around 11:00 a.m. As she looked at her watch, she was amazed to see that it was already 3:45 p.m. and shortly the room would begin to fill with the dinner crowd. Quickly she began to eat so that she could get back into the kitchen and help set up the salad bar.

As Noelle nibbled, the smells wafting from the kitchen, triggered the memories of home. Instantly she thought about her mom and sisters and the times they would share sitting around the table talking about their day. Noelle could feel her heart squeeze in her chest as she remembered how much she enjoyed this time together. She appreciated those times even more now that they were gone. The mind is a funny thing. She could close her eyes and the smells of the wonderful meals that her mom would cook were right there again. With her mouth watering, she could imagine that she was back home. In her ears, she could hear the laughter that they shared. Then her heart would ache as she remembered the sorrow that they felt. She remembered the last three weeks and how her life had taken a different path. Could it be only a few months ago that she was a happy-go-lucky college student whose most pressing concern was her Friday exam and what she was going to wear to that night's party? Yes…the parties they were the start of her fall. She had put herself into situations that could bring her harm. At the time, it seemed like no big deal. She never believed it would lead to this. Yet, here she was! Working vigorously every day trying to prove to the wonderful people who had opened their home to her, that she

1

was not a burden, but an asset. Angelina, Brad and Eyan had proven to be the most amazing family. The love that they had shown to her and her family was beyond anything that Noelle had ever experienced. They were completely giving, totally unselfish and filled with love for all people. Noelle was the recipient of that love. When she thought about what they had already taught her; her heart gripped with emotion and her eyes filled with tears. Thankful did not even begin to express how she felt. Her heart swelled when she thought about how they had offered her more. They had shown her the face of Jesus. God changed her life and now her child will not be a statistic. This child will live. The baby that she carries will breathe life, feel love and have a future with a purpose. It was God's plan that helped her to understand that this baby had to live; had to have a chance to fulfill the spot in this life that God created only for him or her to fill.

"Hey…where are you? You look so lost in thought. Maybe I should let you stay there…or maybe not."

Michelle laughed as she sat down across the table from Noelle with the biggest plate of French fries covered with ground beef, onion and cheese. When she had finished smothering it all with ketchup, she looked up giving Noelle a quizzical look. "What? Ketchup is a vegetable and I need to get 5-8 servings a day…right?" Michelle placed the bottle back onto the table before continuing. "So were you somewhere that you want company?" "I wasn't any place in particular; just thinking about how lucky I am to be here." Noelle shrugged as she continued to eat. She and Michelle had become friends and that was a good thing in this new place. However, she had not shared her secret with Michelle yet; but she knew that soon she would tell her. She wanted to watch their friendship grow more first. This was a secret from her heart with so many elements involved. Noelle needed to know if Michelle cared enough about her to walk this rocky road lovingly before she bared herself more. It was a trust issue. Did Noelle trust Michelle? She had learned the hard way that she had trusted too easily. Now…after what had happened, she was more cautious and their friendship was too new yet. They were working on bonding together and she felt like Michelle was going to become a close friend, maybe even as close as family. Noelle needed family. She was a family person and her family was so far away. She missed them desperately. Angelina and her boys had welcomed her with loving arms into their home. That certainly helped, but Noelle missed the close bond that she had with her sisters and the way that they could discuss everything. It would feel nice to have a female friend her own age that she could share her secrets. Sometimes a girl just needed someone that she could laugh with; someone that could share her tears when they came. Anaya and Nissa had been that to Noelle. They were close enough in age that it had always been the three of them. She could not really remember a time when they were not together. She did not remember her sisters as babies. They had grown together, played together and shared the good and the bad together. When Noelle counted through her friends from home, she realized there was no struggle as she walked away. In fact, there was no one back at home that she would have talked with about that ugly night. On the contrary, she was okay leaving them all behind to guard her family from people like them. She saw up close what her friends at home were really like. When her dad left, she was alone in her pain. In fact, too many times she found two or more of her so-called friends, huddled together in conversations that came to an abrupt end when Noelle

3

entered the room. It was not hard to guess what they had been whispering about…her and her family. Noelle learned quickly to keep her feelings and thoughts to herself. She was not going to share something that would become tomorrow's news around her school and town.

What really bothered her was that she had been one of those people before…before her dad's leaving had rocked her world and caused it to tilt. She had now felt the pain of backbiting, whispered gossip and pitying stares. How could she have done that to someone else? Lesson learned. Never would she allow herself to think that she was better than anyone else. Other people would matter. The person that she used to be had needed to have a face-lift. It did not hurt that through all that had happened she had some "surgery" on her heart. Out with the old and in with the new. She was just learning to depend on the Word of God to instill those new thoughts and ideas. He was teaching her how to be the person that He wanted her life to reflect. It was exciting and she had to admit that she was enjoying finding the person within. Noelle liked who she was becoming. She liked finding herself within His messages. She loved knowing that He loved her.

Every day she was learning how to come away from the wounds of yesterday, and until transformation was complete, she was going to be cautious. Noelle thought to herself, I am going to be patient and watch and see where my relationship with Michelle goes before I let her get too close. She intended to keep a safe distance until she knew Michelle's heart. Her guard would remain up. Michelle on the other hand was an open book and loved to talk. Today was no exception. She began to ramble on about conversations that she had with the lunch crowd. Noelle was beginning to put names

4

to the faces of the regulars that dined at the restaurant.

"And I didn't know that Mrs. Franklin's grandson was just diagnosed with Leukemia. How sad is that? He has been in here so many times with her, such a sweet little boy. His Dad teaches and coaches at the high school about 15 miles north of here. The boy is staying with his grandparents for a few days and they brought him out for lunch."

Noelle thought for a minute and said, "I think that I met him the first week I worked here. Is his name Joey?"

"That's him! Isn't he such a pumpkin? He has the cutest little round pumpkin head and those great big brown eyes. I fell in love the first time that I met him. He is so polite. I think he is 5 years old. He just started kinder-garten last fall. Right now, he is not able to go to school. There is some bug going around in his class and with his immune system compromised, they are being extra care-ful. He was getting a little stir crazy so his grandparents brought him in at the end of the lunch crunch. I felt so bad for him. They made him wear this blue surgical mask over his little face. He could barely get his food in his mouth. He had to work around the mask. It seemed to bother me more than him though." Michelle said.

She continued talking as she ate another fork full of fries, "I heard Angelina say that we're going to do a benefit spaghetti dinner for his fam-ily with a healing service afterwards right here in the restaurant. She is inviting the whole town."

Noelle nodded, "She was talking about it at home. Angelina wants to help so badly." Noelle shook her head and said, "You know what I don't get?"

"What?" Michelle asked.

Pausing Noelle said, "I don't understand why a loving God would want a 5 year old to be sick?"

"Sickness isn't about what God wants. He created us in His image: Body, mind and spirit. But death entered the world through sin when Adam and Eve fell in the garden."

"You make it so matter of fact Michelle. To me, it seems so complicated. There's so much that I just don't understand." Noelle shrugged.

"We live by faith. Peter said that God sent Jesus into this world to bless us. One day I heard a pastor explain it like this, he said the Kingdom of God is a system, not a place, which has come into the earth. Jesus taught us to pray, 'Your will be done, as it is in heaven.' God's will was never that we would be sick and heaven has no sickness. His choice for us would never be sickness. I don't have all of the answers. I do know this, there is no place that we go that God can't change our circumstance or change us during the walk. This life is such a small part of the picture that there is so much we won't understand until we see Him face to face. A wise woman once suggested to me that I make a list of questions that only God can answer for me. I keep that list in my Bible and as I go through day to day every now and then, my experiences find me discovering an answer. I used to be stuck in the questions; now I just wait for Him to lead me to an answer. He always does."

Michelle continued, "Noelle, you will get there. Just keep reading your Bible and asking God to reveal His truth to you. His Holy Spirit living inside of you will make it all clear if you listen for His direction. It seems so complicated; but the truth is, I think that it is so simple that we make it hard. We really don't have to do anything difficult. He did all of the work for us. We just have to follow, because that is what trusting and faith is all about. Just be yourself. God likes you."

"I guess that is the trusting part, how faith comes into all of it. Where sin abounds, there grace abounds even more. It really is about what we are willing to do. He already did His part…right?" Noelle smiled as she thought again, about how far she had come in just a few months. She wondered where she would be in July. It was a thought that danced through her mind daily. There were so many life-changing decisions for her to make. She saw her life like a road map. The most of her life had been on one road. Then came that moment at the crossroads when her dad left their life and her mom and sisters chose to go forward; but Noelle took a turn in the wrong direction. Now the consequences to the choices that she made will stay with her for the rest of her life. Regardless of what she decides to do.

However, she realized that none of the regrets she now had would do one thing to change the past. She compared herself to the Israelites as they roamed around the dessert whining about where they were for 40 years and blaming God for their circumstances. She was not going to do what they did. Noelle believed that until you wanted to solve your problems, you would not. She believed that spiritual obedience was not a choice to take lightly. She knew that she would never forget the past; however, she would look to the past for what it was, a stepping-stone to the future. Through God, she now had a future and she had made a decision to march into that future looking towards the prize that God had given her. Even though she was unsure what that future looked like, she knew if she trusted God He would make a way and that way would look better than anything she could image.

A life…the life of her child…was uncertain before God dropped her into the arms of Angelina and

Brad. Her future, as she had seen it, had been bleak. Life looked different now. She was learning to trust. She was taking baby steps.

Noelle could not help but smile as she thought of the family that had reached out to her. They had not only shared their faith; but had shown her, a perfect stranger with baggage, the love that God had for her.

She was still amazed every time she thought about how lost and alone she was when she left home on her own. How a God, that she never even thought about, if she was going to be honest, guided her direction and brought her straight to a home that chose to be obedient to His Word. Through their love for the Lord, her child would now live. Every day she wondered though, what would her child's future look like?

Where would this baby live? Whose arms would hold and comfort? Would the baby be a boy or girl? Would it be baseballs or dance shoes? Who would watch him or her grow into an adult and be there for the joys and the struggles? Would the baby be better off having Noelle as a mother? On the other hand, under the circumstances, should she give the baby to a family who had empty arms and was desperate to love a child? Was there a perfect family out there that would not care how the baby entered this world?

Noelle's tired mind would go crazy running in circles searching for all of the answers. The answers to these questions would have to be right for both Noelle and the baby. These were the hard answers that they would live with for the rest of their lives.

Noelle noticed the time; stopped her daydreaming and hurried to clean up the table and get back to setting up for the evening meal. Michelle had already left while Noelle was again deep in thought. She must have sensed

8

that Noelle needed a little alone time to battle in her mind.

On her way into the kitchen, Noelle thought about how easy Michelle had made their relationship. She was warm and friendly and the two of them had found that they had a lot in common. Michelle had also come from a divided home. Wow, the first time that Noelle had thought about it that way was a shock to her. She had never really acknowledged that she was one of those statistics. It was almost ridiculous to consider that her family could have joined the ranks of split homes. Really, that did not even fit. Her family had not split. Her dad just wrote a letter that dropped a bomb into the middle of what had appeared to be the perfect family. From the out-side looking in, the appearance was something that every-one else wanted. From the inside looking out, it felt like the best place ever. Dad and Mom loved each other and expressed it openly. She and her two sisters grew up knowing that they were loved, safe and protected from harm.

Little did they know that their dad was living a double life and their life was going to implode? The note he left said he loved someone else and was leaving. That note changed everything. No one knew or could have guessed it was coming. Noelle thought with sarcasm he must have missed his calling. He should have been in movies. His acting skills were impeccable. He had perfected fooling them. Including her mother, who thought that her marriage was all that anybody would want. They were college sweethearts. Their life was full of love. They were raising three beautiful daugh-ters and their future was full of promise. They were the beautiful people that others only hoped to be.

Then one short letter and it all changed. They never saw or talked to him again. Just the check that comes every month through an attorney and a house that doesn't feel like it use to be. It reminds them that he's really gone. They all lost the safe feel of home that one night.

That was one of the reasons that she loved the atmosphere of the restaurant. There was a real sense of family. It was a place to belong. Noelle wanted to belong. She had thrived in that bond of family before her father destroyed their peace.

For now though, she needed to pull herself out of this stroll through the past, as enjoyable as it had been, and get to the rest of the work to be done on her shift. It was time to get back to the kitchen and help set up for the evening crowd. She really loved the work that she had been doing. Working at the restaurant made the day fly. Her day was full so she did not have a lot of time to think about all the decisions that she had to make. She could laugh with people and make sure that their meals were enjoyable. Noelle was beginning to understand why Angelina loved to serve this community. There was a connection. You never knew if today you were going to be able to lighten the load of the next person that walked in to eat. Maybe they needed to have a good laugh or maybe it was just a smile and some peace and quiet after a long day. She was working very hard at trying to become more perceptive to the needs of others. The one think she realized was people loved it when you sincerely cared about how they felt. Noelle made it a point to ask, "How is your day going?" After asking, she really listened to what they had to say.

It was becoming clear to her there were so many burdened people who just needed someone to care. Angelina always said, "If you can help someone in the course of their day to feel better, it makes your problems seem so much less. We are not here to pass through, but to serve. So serve with all of your heart. Sometimes all that they need is a friendly face and a listening ear. That is service too."

Angelina was right. If you looked, you could see when someone came in with a heavy heart. Nothing felt better than when you were able to see that burden start to lift; see it replaced with a smile on their face.

What surprised Noelle was that she could make them laugh. She had never thought of herself as funny. Now she was realizing that she could be entertaining. She could be quite the comedian. Just that thought alone made her laugh and laughing lightened the load on her day.

The kitchen was a flurry of activity as Noelle entered and began gathering the supplies out of the walk-in refrigerator that they would need on the salad bar. As she started to push the swinging exit door, Angelina came up and gave her a quick hug. "How are you doing Honey? Is everything okay with your day? Do you need some down time?" she asked.

Noelle was quick to answer, "I'm fine. I just sat down and ate a salad with Michelle. I'm ready to go; anxious to get the dinner crowd under way. Am I doing everything that you want me to do? Please don't feel like you can't correct me if you need to. I want to be treated just like everyone else and I want to do a great job for you."

Angelina laughed. "Oh, there aren't going to be any special favors for you. No sir! I'm going to ride you harder than anybody else; no free rides for you. I'll make sure that you keep your nose to the grindstone; and all that stuff. There is no reason for you to get special treatment. You are going to work, work, work; practically slave labor. Why I'm going to...." "Enough already! I get it. It's okay if you want to ask me how my day is going. I will stop trying to prove to you that

11

I am not sponging off you. I just want to do a good job to repay your kindness. Maybe I'm a little sensitive about that okay?" Noelle laughed and so did Angelina.

"You're doing a wonderful job. The diners love you. I get nothing but great compliments. Relax and enjoy. Work never seems like work if you like what you do. As tired as I can be when I go home at night, it never feels like drudgery. I love what I do and I love the people who walk through that door, whether I know them or not. I know that for whatever time they are here, God has dropped them into my life and given me the opportunity to serve them. It feels good to let God use you. Now, let's get going. We've a dinner meal to get ready for." Angelina gave her a quick hug and was off.

As Noelle readied the salad bar, she noticed that Angelina checked in with each of her staff. She was always so attentive to their needs. Mothering. That was what she did so naturally. It made Noelle stop and ask herself, *Could I be that kind of a mother? One who just naturally loves regardless of the situation? Would I be able to look at my newborn baby and love unconditionally? Could I look into those baby eyes and never feel resentment for the ugly conception? Would the past be gone; or would I be haunted every time that sweet face looked at me?* Noelle knew she had to find an answer for the questions that continued to haunt the recesses of her mind. Could she forget? Could she forget…and forgive? No child deserved to carry that burden for life. She could only keep this baby if she could get past that night, the night that defined this pregnancy for her. Could she forget the night when someone gave her drugs in her drink and changed everything for her? Could she forget waking up the next morning in the bed of someone that she did not even know? She had to be able to let that go. On

12

the other hand, would the baby be a constant reminder of that night? Would she remember her mistakes for the rest of that child's life? Could she forget and still love? That question crept into her thoughts on a regular basis.

For now, she would stick it into the deep recesses of her mind and focus on the task.

By the time that she got the salad bar all set up, the rooms were beginning to fill with people young and old. The evening went so quickly that she hardly realized that it was over. Only the nagging reminders from feet that were aching from standing on them all day and legs that felt like they had run miles through the course of the night. It was a good feeling though. The restaurant had been full all evening. People were out shopping. There were extra families stopping in after watching a drama program at the local high school. Many grandparents had come out to admire their grandchildren's performances on stage and boast about their young stars. Because of the program, there were more large groups tonight. Noelle did not mind that. Usually the tips were more with groups. She could always use more money.

As the crew cleaned up the rooms, Angelina and the kitchen staff were putting everything in order and getting ready for the morning shift to come in. The staff spread the leftover food out on the tables for Angelina's restaurant family to eat. She always made sure they got a good meal before they went home for the night. It was after 10:00 p.m. by the time that the last customer left. Starving, they sat and ate together laughing about all that had happened during the day. It was this time of the work day when they had their conversations about any changes that they would need to make for the morning and Angelina was quick to thank everyone for all that they had done during their shifts. Noelle loved this time together. The camaraderie felt good. It was this type of closeness that made Angelina's staff want to work so hard for her.

When everyone was full, they cleaned up after themselves, wiped down the table, checked the floors and said one last good-bye for the night. The morning shift would open and set up for breakfast. Most of this crew would not be back until either the lunch or the dinner shift.

Noelle had ridden in with Angelina that morning so she helped her close up. It made for a long day. Over twelve hours had gone by since they had walked into the restaurant. It was a good day and being tired helped Noelle to sleep better through the night. Otherwise, so many questions would run repeatedly through her mind. No…tired was better.

In the car, they talked about what the day had brought. Noelle told Angelina about some of the people that she had met that day. They were so friendly and welcoming. Angelina tried to fill Noelle in on the basics. Who was related to whom or how many kids they had? Angelina would say, "Oh they grew up here or that family is one of our transplants. We were just lucky that they chose our little town to put down roots." Noelle was beginning to see them as families and not just faces.

"Now are you sure that you're not trying to work too many hours?" Angelina asked. "After all, you need to take care of yourself too."

"I'm fine. I like working. Although, I did call that doctor that you recommended and I have an appointment for next week Monday. The only time that I could get in was at 1:30. I hope that isn't going to cause you too much trouble. I will probably miss the whole lunch shift. I'm guessing I will have to leave the restaurant around 12:30 to make sure that I can find the place on time. I have

14

no idea where I'm going in Indianapolis." Noelle said.

"Stop it. We are not going to worry about that. I am just glad you got an appointment. So will your mom. Are you okay going by yourself? I could take the morning off and go with you if you would like?"

"No, I'll be okay. You would have to rear-range your schedule and you are already going to be short one with me gone. I will just come straight to the restaurant after my appointment so that I can help with the dinner shift. I am so sorry that all of this is playing out the way that it is. You will already be short with me leaving on Wednesday and now I will be gone half of Monday too." Noelle finished.

"Now stop fussing about all of that. We are going to be fine and you are going to have a wonderful time with your family. Just know that if you don't want to go to this appointment alone, I'll be there with you." Angelina patted Noelle's leg as she finished. She was feeling very sneaky knowing the secret that she was keeping.

"Thank you so much. It's nice to know that if I need someone, you're willing to be there." They finished the conversation as they pulled into the farm.

There was that flutter again. Noelle was always surprised when she felt it. The flutter that happened when she saw that Brad's truck was home. It was always nice to have a few minutes to chat with him before going to bed. She was beginning to realize that she looked forward to that part of her day. Noelle loved those few minutes of sitting together on the couch and sharing what had happened during their day. They didn't sit for very long. Still it was always a nice ending to a long day.

Brad met them at the door and took the bags that the girls were carrying. Angelina quickly gave a few instructions and said good night. She wanted to leave for the restaurant in the morning by 9:30 sharp. With that said, she was off to bed leaving them alone.

Noelle smiled shyly at Brad, "Hi how was your day?"

"It was just a usual day; nothing out of the ordinary. You're the best thing by far that's come my way today." He replied with a sheepish grin.

As much as she loved his teasing, she tried not to take him too seriously. After all, what could Brad Conroy see in someone in her situation? She had to guard her heart. If she didn't guard her heart, she could see it shattering.

Brad recognized that look. He saw it every time that he attempted to flirt with her. He was sure that he understood where it was coming from. She was emotionally fragile. Like a butterfly working its way out of a cocoon. He knew that he had to let her work her way out. The struggle of becoming free was the only way that she would learn to stand on her own. His instinct was to help. However, if he did that, she could be damaged for life and never learn how to fly.

Brad wanted Noelle to fly. He wanted her to soar on wings like eagles. It was a promise from God to her.

Isaiah 40:31
But those who hope in the Lord
will renew their strength.
They will soar on wings like eagles;
they will run and not grow weary,
they will walk and not be faint

He knew that if she could get her bearing, together they could make the world a better place. He also knew Noelle was the woman that God was preparing for him and he was a patient man. Brad knew that Noelle's problems were not going to be an easy fix for her. He also knew that she had not completely learned to trust God and that God

16

was the only fixer. Yes, Noelle had trusted God for her salvation; but trusting Him for the every day, a minute-by-minute decision was a process. There was so much that he wanted to say to her when the time was right. One thing was sure, she had to make some hard decisions in the next few months and he did not want her to base those decisions on what he said or did not say. Brad knew what he wanted her to decide. He had already come to grips with where he stood on the baby. He was in love with the mother and God was already preparing his heart for the day that he would hold that little one. Someday, after she had made up her mind about what she needed to do, he hoped that they would get a chance to work through all of that together. But not now. Not until the time was right. Brad rested in the knowledge that if God was preparing his heart, He was also preparing Noelle's heart.

"Well, maybe I'll see you in the morning. I think that I am going up to bed. It has been a long day." Noelle smiled as she headed for the stairs.

"No cup of tea with me tonight?" Brad asked.

"I don't think so; not tonight. Tomorrow morning is early and I don't want to make your mom late. Thanks though." Noelle started up the stairs wondering why she had refused his offer. Turning, she looked back as she started up the landing and saw that Brad was still watching her with a smile on his face.

"Good night Noelle." He said. "Sleep tight."

"Good night." She smiled as she answered back and stepped out of his sight. Walking up the steps to her room, she could still see his dimpled smile in her mind. The flutter danced its way across her heart one more time.

Chapter Two

Psalm 96:2

Sing to the Lord,

praise His name;

Proclaim His alvation

day after day.

ANGELINA LAY IN BED CONTEMPLATING HER NEW charge. Noelle could not have met her expectations of a new employee any better than she had. In fact, she was an over achiever. She worked tirelessly from morning to night. That was the problem. Noelle was trying so hard to prove her worth to Angelina that she was going to burn out from exhaustion. Then what would she tell Noelle's mother; whom she talked to on a regular basis. It was not that she didn't understand. She did. She understood it all too well. When your life changes direction and that direction is not for the better; somewhere deep inside you have to prove to the world that you are good enough. Even worse, you begin trying to prove to yourself that you are still you. It becomes crucial that you understand for yourself that you are good enough. You have to know that the circumstance that you now find yourself in has not altered the person that you thought you were. For Noelle that translated into showing Angelina how hard she could work and how responsible she was. Angelina figured that Noelle desperately needed to prove she was not the kind of girl who would get herself into a situation where she could end up pregnant and desperate.

What Angelina understood, and Noelle had not come to grips with yet, was any one of us on any given day could find ourselves caught in the snares of satan if we let our guard down. For that reason, we need to be in the Word daily renewing our minds and preparing for the battle that rages around us. Angelina wanted Noelle to understand without a doubt that we are all capable of sin. That is why we needed a Savior. Without Jesus, we are hopeless; with Him, there is love and protection.

There were so many similarities between Angelina and Noelle that it was scary. In so many ways, she could relate to the things that Noelle did; the type "A" personality that ran full speed ahead wanting to be in charge. For Noelle right now that was so hard to do when everything seemed to be spinning out of control and she couldn't stop it. With so much weighing upon her shoulders and so many questions to find answers to, the road ahead was rocky, to say the least, for Noelle if she tried to walk it by herself. Only by letting go and letting the God of the universe take the lead, would she find the *"peace that passes all understanding."*

The fact that Noelle was a baby Christian made this all the more difficult for her. The answers would be so much easier to find if the knowledge of the Bible could be poured into Noelle. That would be too easy. God wants us digging to find Him. He loves when we are hungry and seeking after Him in an active way. He is all about relationship with us. God wants us hungry for Him. Angelina could almost hear the conversations circling through the little girl's head continually. There were those down times when she would finally see her stop to grab a quick bite between shifts at the restaurant. Instantly you could see that far away look. You just knew she was inside her head mulling over question after question. No doubt about it, these were going to be tough questions with tough answers; questions only Noelle could seek for the answers. Angelina was thankful the option of abortion was off the table. Yet, she still was amazed at how the Lord had orchestrated Noelle's life and brought her right here to this home. He truly is amazing in how He loves. It made Angelina think about the "Parable of the Lost Sheep" and how the Bible tells that Noelle's Angel in Heaven always sees the face of the Father.

Angelina Grabbed her Bible from her bedside table and looked up the scripture in *Matthew 18:12-14.*

"What do you think? If a man owns a hundred sheep, and one of them wanders away, will he not leave the ninety-nine on the hills and go to look for the one that wandered off? And if he finds it, I tell you the truth, he is happier about that one sheep than about the ninety-nine that did not wander off. In the same way your Father in heaven is not willing that any of these little ones should be lost."

She served that God, a God who was not willing to let go of Noelle. He loved her so much, He directed her path hundreds of miles so that she could end up in a spot where she would hear about His love for her and for her unborn child. We are all fortunate enough to be loved by a Father that much.

Although…if Angelina was being completely honest, watching Noelle walk through this journey had certainly stirred up those memories from the past, the ones that had been vanished from the present for so long. Angelina would not have chosen to re-walk this path. As far as the east is from the west, that part of her life was gone. That was what God had done for her. He had carried her burden. There had been forgiveness a long time ago. God had wiped the slate clean, seeing her white as snow.

It was not that Angelina was taking back the ugliness of despair or regret; it was just that she understood all too well the pain and suffering of having to make those kinds of decisions. She remembered those feelings of loneliness and desperation. This she knew, only Noelle could make the decisions that loomed ahead in her future. Only Noelle would have to live with them deep in her heart.

Watching Noelle brought back the memories of the path she chose when she was Noelle's age. The loneliness and the feeling that she had no other option could still resurface from the back recesses of her mind. Memories that had been buried for years became so real today she could feel every emotion from the past coming forward. The reality of what had been told to her. "It is not a baby. It is just a mass of cells." If only she had talked with someone who could have given her truth. If she could have seen an ultra-sound that showed a real life developing inside of her. If only she had stopped long enough to allow God to reassure her that He was still in control and He knew the way. She had not. She moved forward swiftly and quickly. She walked into that abortion clinic by herself. The broken girl that she was followed the orders of the staff there. The uncontrollable sobbing, the sadness that engulfed her, the sounds of that machine sucking the life of her unborn child out of her; those were the memories that left with her that day. She had remembered them for years. They consumed her thoughts day and night. Too often, she would wake up in the middle of the night screaming. The hours that she spent on her knees pleading with God for His forgiveness and mercy did not stop until she found a group of Intercessory Prayer Counselors who helped her walk through the forgiveness that only God could bring into her life. They helped her to understand she could beg for God's forgiveness forever; yet, she still needed to accept it on a personal basis. God could only go so far and then Angelina would need to meet Him. He would carry her burden for her. She still had to let Him have it and not take it back. They taught her that God had already forgiven her through the stripes that His Son took for her on the road to the cross. His blood had already paid the price for her forgiveness. Yet, her healing had to come from her forgiving herself. She had to be able to accept the healing that God's plan of redemption offered.

Then there was Terran. The most gentle, loving man she had ever known. He had loved her right where she was. He looked at her heart and saw the brokenness. Through him, she saw love, support, and an encouragement to follow Christ. His patience never wavered, even when the depression from the past would set in. She thought of it as her 'crazy cycle'. It was vicious and was a reoccurring place that she lived. She tried so hard to stuff the ugliness of that day away. Angelina wanted the memories to stop. However, they came, sometimes in floods. She would lock herself away in her bedroom and cry for hours. Terran would hold her and rock her gently as he told her, "Let it go. Jesus does not want you living in this pain. He just wants you to trust Him. He will take all of your pain away."

Slowly Angelina began to understand satan did not want her living a life of freedom. He had her in his grips. As long as he could keep her punishing herself for the abortion, he could keep her from fulfilling the mission that God had planned for her.

When she was finally able to accept that God had already forgiven her, that her forgiveness came the day that Jesus climbed onto that cross, then she was finally able to close the door on the sorrow that engulfed her life. She began to see how the lies of the enemy had kept her in bondage for years.

It was a slow process. She would have to remind herself frequently she did not have to remember that day. It was a choice she made to tell the enemy no! He could not manipulate her mind anymore.

The counselor suggested that she name her baby. She named her Eden; it meant a place of pleasure. She did that because she liked to think of the baby being with Jesus and walking with Him hand in hand in the cool of the day. She saw the two of them united in fellowship together. It brought her pleasure to think of the baby that way: To visualize Jesus holding her baby while they waited for the time when Angelina would be able to wrap Eden in her arms and love her the way that she wished she could everyday since the abortion.

She had found healing in the arms of Jesus, both for her and for her baby. From her time of healing forward, her life changed and so did the life she built with Terran. Shortly after her heaing, they began to think about starting their family together. Looking back, she was glad that they had waited. She was a better mother when she loved herself through the heart of Jesus instead of through the shattered pieces of her own heart. She treasured her life with the boys and they never knew the person that she thought she was before she really accepted the love and forgiveness of Jesus.

God knows we cannot live on the mountain top experiences. Into every life, rain will fall and there will be valleys. How we walk through the valleys determines how we will be able to see the heart of God. He has never called us to live in guilt or shame. Angelina knew when she was broken and emotionally empty; she was not able to help herself. In that condition, it was impossible for her to help anyone else either. It was only after she began to live in the love of the Savior that she could be available to help someone else. She had to recognize Jesus for who He was. He was willing to do all of the heavy lifting for her. Before He could drop broken people into her life for help, she had to be able to see the world as it was, God's world. The world He created where His people would interact with people who were broken and needed to feel His love.

From the moment she accepted His healing forgiveness, Angelina vowed that she would live her life looking at the world as Jesus sees it. Jesus did not wait for us to come to Him; He came to us. Through the life of a little baby, hope for the future was brought to life. We just have to be willing to see through His eyes. We cannot fix the world; but we can fix the ones that He puts in front of us. Again, only if we are looking through the eyes of Jesus will we see it as it really is. Seeing through His eyes can change it. Our Savior is everywhere calling us to look. There are broken people everywhere in desperate need of some hope. Who is going to tell them if God's people look broken too?

Angelina pressed closer and closer to God over the years. She was always looking to be obedient to the Lord. It became second nature for her to ask God to bring the broken to her. Then the call from Brad that day brought Noelle.

As Angelina drove home that night Matthew 25 was running through her head. It was the scripture where Jesus is telling the parable of the sheep and the goats. *"He will separate the people one from another as a shepherd separates the sheep from the goats. He will put the sheep on his right and the goats on his left.*

Then the King will say to those on his right, 'Come, you who are blessed by my Father; take your inheritance, the kingdom prepared for you since the creation of the world. For I was hungry and you gave me something to eat, I was thirsty and you gave me something to drink, I was a stranger and you invited me in. I

25

needed clothes and you clothed me, I was sick and you looked after me, I was in prison and you came to visit me.

Then the righteous will answer him, 'Lord, when did we see you hungry and feed you, or thirsty and give you something to drink? When did we see you a stranger, invite you in or needing clothes, and clothe you? When did we see you sick or in prison and go to visit you?

The King will reply, 'I tell you the truth, whatever you did for one of the least of these brothers of mine, you did for me.'

Angelina remembered thinking, help me to discern what her needs are Father and equip me to meet them. Little did she know what the Father was going to ask of her. With this broken young woman, God was going to ask her to brush away the cob webs of her life in the area that Angelina thought was sealed shut. He was going to give her the perfect opportunity to open up the door to the past and share her walk. It was not an easy decision to go there. She had never talked about that day with anyone. Not even Terran had asked her to relive the ugliness that had happened. Yet, God would not ask her to go where He would not lead. She knew that God was going to wake up the part of her that wanted to remain quiet. She also knew that was her most dangerous spot. To stay quiet and miss the calling opportunity that God had provided for her, would only keep her from seeing His face and walking in the blessing that He had waiting for her. She knew she could have turned away. God would not have condemned her for doing so. She also knew He had offered her a place to minister. The call to movement was her decision. So…she went, hard as it was, she went. The saving grace was, this baby would live and she felt like Eden had played a part in making that difference. In addition, wasn't this what God had prepared her for? Hadn't He given her the knowledge and tools through her walk to help Noelle? That had been her opportunity to make a difference in His kingdom and to be obedient to His calling.

Still, Angelina's heart broke for Noelle and she knew the best thing she could do to help was pray; and so she did.

Dearest Father, I lift up Noelle to you again. Your word tells us to pray unceasingly. I beg You to give Your daughter the answers that she is seeking. I pray peace will wash over her as Your will for her life becomes so clear she cannot miss Your direction.

Father help her to forgive the young man who played a part in this wherever he is. Help her to understand that only through forgiveness can she be free. Open his eyes to the heartache his choices are making. Put someone in his life to speak the gospel to him and help him to change his life for the better.

Father I see the look in my son's eyes. I know that look. He is falling in love with this girl. Guard his heart. If it be Your will for this connection, then make a way for them to find a perfect start in a not so perfect situation. Only you can do that.

Brad has the heart of a compassionate man. Give him the patience that he will need to wait on Noelle's decisions and the serenity to wait on You. Father we all need You to walk with us through this. Be with Noelle's family as they are separated at this very difficult time. Your word says that, "everything has a season." Let this season pass quickly for her and her family and find a way to bring them back together again. In Jesus Name. Amen.

With that done, Angelina thought about the conversations she had been having with Noelle's mother, Genie. She was so excited about the surprise that they were planning for Noelle. In just a few days

Genie and Noelle's sisters, Nissa and Anaya, would be arriving to spend a few days here at the farm. This Saturday they were leaving to come for a visit. The best part was that without Noelle even knowing, she had scheduled her first ultra sound and they will be here to go with her. Their plan is to get here by Sunday night and Noelle had just told her that she would see the doctor on Monday. Angelina could not wait to call Genie tomorrow morning and tell her how that was working out.

Angelina knew they were all so sad Noelle was going through this struggle without them by her side. Being able to share her first appointment would make them so happy. Plus…she was sure it was going to mean the world to Noelle as well. She would call them first thing in the morning.

✱✱✱✱✱✱✱✱✱✱✱✱✱✱✱✱

Across town, Michelle lay in her bed with a jumble of thoughts running through her head. She was really enjoying getting to know Noelle. However, there was something distant about her. Michelle was sure that there was an area of her life that she kept bottled up. Too many times, she would find her deep in thought. The look on her face would show the weight of a burden that she was carrying.

Michelle knew that look. Too many times in her old life she had carried secrets; secrets that burdened her all the way to her soul. She will always remember the day that she was shown the light and the weight of the world was lifted from her shoulders. August 22, 2010. Her mind went back to that moment in her life when everything changed. That was the day that she became a new creation. As sleep eluded her, she easily drifted back and began to retrace the steps of that life-changing day.

The day was balmy; there was a pleasant feel to the morning. However, Michelle was not in the mood to feel pleasant. The night before had been rough. She had barely slept. The cramping had been so bad for the last few days that all she wanted to do was try to sleep the pain away. It was not working. She had already taken the pain pills that the clinic had given to her after the procedure. There should not have been this kind of pain. She knew. She had been here before. This was her second time walking through this. Not that she was proud of that. In fact, it left her feeling sick inside. How did she get into this place in her life? Looking in the mirror, she did not even recognize the person that looked back. This was not who she had set out to be. Where did it all go wrong? If she asked that question honestly, it would be where did she go wrong? How had she allowed her life to turn in this direction; a direction that had only brought her heartache and despair?"

Her life had never been wonderful. She was the only child of a single mom and never knew who her dad was. Her mom refused to talk about it. Until one day, a day just like any other day, when her mom had been drinking, Michelle pushed and pushed. In a rage, her mother yelled at her, "You want me to say it…Okay…I don't know who your 'daddy' was. I was sleeping with so many guys during that time that it could have been anyone. But…it doesn't matter. None of them would have been good to you. They weren't quality. If you know what I mean."

Saying that, her mother slammed the door and walked out leaving Michelle alone to process everything that she had said. It wasn't a surprise to her that her mom had been that person. She wasn't naive to what was happening in her home as she grew up. The question was, "Who did that make Michelle now?" The answer was, "she didn't know." Her gene pool wasn't looking very promising.

That night she cried herself to sleep. She felt like she was a nobody. Had anybody ever really wanted her? There had never been grandparents in her life. Now she began to wonder why. Her mom had always told her that it was just the two of them. Was that true? Were there family members that were out there that would love her? If so, she wanted to meet them. It was scary having only one person in your life. The thoughts were always there; wonderings about what would happen to her if all of a sudden her mom was gone. Who would be there for her? Would she be all alone? Michelle was only 14. She did not want to be totally alone. She wanted to have someone who really loved her and wanted to take care of her. That was something she had never known. Michelle's mom had never nurtured her.

It was not that her mom did not love her. She knew that she did. Even though she was not very good at showing it or saying, "I love you". Michelle could count on one hand the times that she had heard those words. Always it was because she had asked over and over, "Do you love me?" Then, just like today, her mom would yell the words at her and then she was gone. Never had her mom sat and lovingly stroked her hair or hugged her close and said the words that Michelle was so desperate to hear, "I love you. You're so precious to me."

After that night, Michelle began to feel like she was totally on her own to find the love that she craved. So she began looking. She would find herself anywhere someone would wrap their arms around her and say nice things about her. She was looking to fill a huge hole in her heart with love. She just did not know what real love felt like. Michelle embarked on a rocky trip. Ugly details that she did not want to remember. The road that she was on never led to anywhere very pretty. Two abortions later here she was waking up to the same old life, with the same old problems. Only this time they were intensifying.

This morning was different from the first time. Michelle knew that she did not want to be on this path any more. The problem was, she did not even know how to get off this crazy cycle that she was on. Here she was lying in pain, alone and desperate without her mother to talk to. She had not seen her mother since the night she barely graduated from high school.

She knew she had not been the easiest child; but her mother had not been the best mom.

Graduation night was the end for their relationship, if you could call what they had a relationship? Her mom showed up at her ceremony drinking. This was not unusual. She never was without the smell of alcohol on her breath. That night was different. Her mom was exceptionally loud and obnoxious. After the ceremony, when the families all gathered, she found her mom with the current man of choice waiting off to the side. Michelle was ashamed for anyone to know that person belonged to her. She was standoffish, which her mom must have perceived as Michelle thinking she was too good to be seen with her. Her mother made a scene and told her that she had done her job now and Michelle needed to get out and find her own life. She continued by telling her that she was going to be gone for a week. She said, "Get your stuff packed up and be gone by the time that I get back." Then she handed her $200.00 and said, "Well, congratulations you did more than I could; even though I wondered if you would ever make it. At least you did. Well…have a great life"

Turning to her friend her mother said, "Let's go. She will be fine. She never needed me anyway." And she left.

Michelle thought about how the story did not get any better from there on until the day when she found herself in pain and desperation.

She would always remember seeing the blood as it covered the sheets. Panicked she knew that she was in real trouble. Michelle stumbled out into the hall and down the stairs. Not thinking clearly, she decided to walk. For the rest of her life she would wonder how she ever got to the hospital. Whoever helped her, saved her life. She spent a couple of day there while they worked to bring her body back to health. One surgery later and lots of blood pumped into her, she lived.

However, that became the best thing that ever happened to her. While she was in the hospital, a Chaplain stopped by to see her. Seeing her in desperate need, he connected her with a women's shelter that took her under their wing. Through that group of women she found Jesus and that started her on the path to a new life.

These women taught her about the love that she had been craving forever. They gave her a Bible and she could not put it down. Every day she found something new in her Savior's word that brought her more and more healing. She even began to realize that she had to forgive her mother to find true peace in her life. That was what she needed. She wanted the *"peace that passes all understanding."* Michelle also learned that God is not a God of disorder, but of order and peace.

Her life had been out of order since the beginning. For the first time, she was realizing that there was more and it did not involve living a life of sin. Michelle found a Father who loved her. She learned that if she went to Him, He would come to her. Finding this new life, she went and went and went. It was the safest most loving place she had ever had and through it, she found the peace that she had always craved.

Michelle treasured the memory of the day that a well-meaning woman said to her, "Now you are a sinner saved by grace."

Answering politely Michelle corrected her, "No ma'am. Now I am a new creation. Jesus does not see me as a sinner anymore. She believed this in her heart and this message had changed her life forever.

Therefore, if anyone is in Christ, he is a new creation; the old has gone, the new has come!
II Corinthians 5:17

Michelle had grabbed a hold of the lifeline and that lifeline was Jesus Christ. The solution for every-thing that was wrong in her life was the Cross. The devil had stolen the early years of her life from her and she now understood that God wanted to give back to her ev-erything that she had lost. He was waiting and all that she had to do was reach out, grab Him by faith. She had begun the walk of pursuing God with all of her heart.

Michelle wanted to share all of this with Noelle. She wanted her to know that she did not have to carry a burden. Michelle wanted Noelle to under-stand that Jesus loved her more than she could imag-ine. She had a Heavenly Father, and He did not want her to walk shackled. She knew that Noelle had ac-cepted Jesus as her Savior. There was so much more and Michelle wanted to help Noelle find the kind of love and contentment that was waiting for her.

She had realized that unless you are pursuing God with all your heart, you could be disappointed with Christianity. Walking by faith is about losing your life so you can connect with the purpose that God has for you.

"And you will seek Me and find Me, when you search
for Me with all your heart."
Jeremiah 29:13

She once heard a pastor speak of it as having a "wholehearted devotion to God." Michelle
thought that was a perfect description. God wants all
of you. Otherwise, it will feel like you have lost something, like something is missing and you want it back.

You shall love the Lord your God with all your heart,
with all your soul, and with all your mind."
Matthew 22:37

Seeking God with only half of your heart will
never bring you the kind of joy or peace that you were
created to have. Michelle had spent all of her early life
trying to find that kind of love; the kind of love that only
comes through a Father that would lay down His life for
you. That is what she found when she found Jesus. The
women at the shelter taught her that God loved her so
much, the God she did not know, that He sent His son
to die a horrendous death on a cross for her. That He
willingly suffered a beating and still went to that cross,
carrying the weight of all of her sins on his shoulders. He
willingly crawled up on that cross and laid there while
they drove nails into his hands and feet. He did that for her.

In doing that, He made these commitments
to her. He was saying that He would never leave her
and that He would supply all of her needs. He would
listen to her prayers and then answer. The answers
may not be what she was looking for; but she believed
that they would always be what were best for her.

From the cross, He was saying that
He would forgive all of her sins…all of
them. The sins of her past would be no more.
He promised to give her a spiritual gift and

the ability to use it well. All she had to do was trust that He would never call her into anything she was not equipped. She just had to be willing to go where He led.

He promised that He would give her the Holy Spirit to guide and direct her life. She discovered that when God begins to move through you, your perspective changes.

The best part was that He was preparing a place in Heaven for her so that when her life on earth was over, He would take her to live with Him for eternity.

The women in the shelter spoke volumes into her heart and they helped her to heal from the burdens of the abortions. She walked through grief counseling where she began to forgive her mother. Then she began to forgive herself for taking the lives of her unborn children. They helped her to understand that God knew she was a new creation and that the choices of her old life were behind her. She did not have to look back any more. There was a new road for her to walk and she did not have to walk it in the dark.

I have come into the world as a light, so that no one who believes in me should stay in darkness.
John 1:46

Michelle discovered as she began to understand the Jesus that loved her, there was a difference in the way she wanted to live her life. She had a desire to obey and serve Him. As she learned more about Him, she wanted to share this love of her life with others. When she read the Bible, she trusted His love for her more and more. She learned how to worship Him and could not wait for her time alone with Him. Meditating on His word brought her pleasure and He became a real part of her life. Michelle realized that she would never be happy without Him in her life. It was as if she had been set free from a prison and now she could love others with the love that she had always wanted in her life.

As she finally began to doze off her last request was to her Heavenly Father.

Dear God will you please open the door so that I can share your message of peace with Noelle? Your love makes everything better. It's me, your daughter Michelle, and I love you God. Good night and Amen.

With those words of love spoken, Michelle slipped into a peaceful sleep and dreamed of beauty and the love of the best daddy ever.

Chapter Three

Psalm 96:3

Declare His glory among the nations,

His marvelous deeds among all peoples.

MORNING AGAIN? GENIE WAS EXHAUSTED AFTER another long night of tossing and turning. Lying in her bed, which had always seemed so comfortable, as had her whole life, she wondered to herself, why is it so impossible for me to sleep well. Am I destined to do this for the rest of my life? She hoped this was not going to be her new pattern; however, lying there alone, she couldn't help but question herself, why not? Just like the rest of her life had changed, so had her sleeping pattern. As usual, the thoughts just circled and circled in her head. Last night there were too many questions going through her mind about her oldest daughter. She was sure that some relief would come when Noelle finally saw the doctor. There was reassurance in having a doctor tell her that everything was progressing as expected. At 20 weeks, they should be scheduling an ultrasound. For some reason, Genie felt like Noelle was dragging her feet on making that appointment, yet as her mother, she was anxious for that to happen. An ultrasound would show her that all was well. There would be a picture of little toes and fingers. Maybe the baby would be sucking his or her thumb. A picture of contentment wrapped snuggly in mommy's womb. It could not be soon enough for Genie. She needed to know that Noelle and the baby were both okay. She could not wait until she and the girls could surprise her. Noelle thought that she was coming home for spring break and that was the original plan. However, Angelina was so adamant that they should come to Indiana. Genie had to admit that she was anxious to be back in the Conroy home. There was such a feeling of peace and contentment. Since Gale had left, every night sleep normally eluded her. Yet while she had been at the Conroy home, she had slept like a baby. Genie was sure that part of it was that she knew Noelle was safe and just having the ability to physically put her hands on her daughter was reassuring. There was underlying peace in their home that somehow made you feel like everything was okay. Genie was desperate for more of that kind of peace.

She had been reading the Bible that Angelina and Brad had given her. It did help. Yet, she had to admit that there was so much that she did not understand. Angelina would be the perfect person to help her answer some of those questions. She and the girls had been church shopping ever since Noelle had left. Nothing had felt like home. The girls were just as eager as she was to find that perfect fit. They were looking for different things so it needed to be a church that offered diversity. They needed a place with an active youth group; but she would like a woman's group that would help her to grow into who God wanted her to be. She knew that there was just the right spot for them somewhere. They would just keep looking. She was sure they would find it because they had begun to trust in God's divine direction in their lives. She and the girls were praying about this together. God would answer their prayers, and they would feel it when it was right.

Nevertheless, for today it was time to move. So out of bed she jumped and headed for the shower. She liked to have breakfast ready by the time that Nissa and Anaya came down to the kitchen. That way they could have a little time to read their morning devotional together while they ate. They had all picked this book out at the Christian bookstore in town and they really loved starting their day with God as a family. They had bought

40

two books so that Noelle would have one with her also. Sometimes they would get into discussions with Noelle in the evening. If it was not too late and she was not too tired, she always tried to call after she got home from work.

"Hi Mom! Anaya chimed as she entered the kitchen. "Nissa is running a little late." She said, "Don't start without her. She'll be right here."

"Okay. We have time to wait." Genie answered giving her youngest daughter a quick morning hug.

"No waiting," Nissa yelled from the stairs. "I'm ready." She said as she came charging into the kitchen.

Genie laughed at the thought that they were so eager in the morning. Neither of them had ever been morning people. She recalled the mornings of grumbling and prodding to see that they were not late. She thought about the scripture that she had just read before going to bed last night

"Listen girls" Genie, eager to share, said, "I read this last night and it reminded me of you two,

'they will soar on wings like eagles, they will run and not grow weary, they will walk and not be faint.'
I love that you two plow down those stairs in the mornings now."

"I think that I read that in Isaiah 40," Nissa said.

"So good morning my little eagles!" Genie giggled at the expression of silliness on the girls' faces.

Nissa said, "Want to know why I was almost late? I called Noelle this morning and woke her up." She wrinkled her nose at the protest that her mother was about to make. "I know…But I just wanted to hear her voice. We did not talk much yesterday, although she did not say much this morning. She was sleepy. I just told her that we miss her and

41

cannot wait until she gets here during spring break. Then I laughed to myself. I was pretty sneaky huh?"

Genie scolded with a loving tone, "Now don't you girls let the surprise slip. The look on her face when we get there will be the best present that I could receive."

"Oh Mom!" The girls chimed in. "We aren't going to blow the surprise."

Anaya started to laugh as she said, "Remember when we kept the secret about the diamond earrings that Dad bought…." She stopped in midstream as she realized what she had just said. Instantly an uneasy quiet filled the room.

"Now stop it." Genie said. "We can't pretend like our life just started right now. It did not. We have many wonderful memories and we are not going to erase them because things have changed. Besides, how can we know that God wants us to forgive others and not practice that forgiveness with your father?"

"I'm sorry. It just slipped out. I don't want it to be harder for you. Plus, I am not sure that I am ready to practice my forgiveness on him. Maybe I will be someday…just not yet. I think that it's enough that I try praying for him." Anaya finished.

"That's alright. At least it is a start. A few weeks ago, we were not even doing that. We are making progress…right?" Genie smiled at the girls.

"That's right Mom." Anaya said.

Things settled in as they opened their devotional and Nissa began to read. As they ate, they talked about their morning Bible scripture and they had just finished when the phone rang.

Genie saw the caller ID. "It's Angelina." She said as she answered the phone. "Good morning."

"Good morning to all of you. Are you all there

42

by any chance? I was hoping to catch you together." Angelina said.

"We are. Is everything all right?" Genie took a hesitant breath as she put the phone on speaker.

"Oh yes. In fact, it is better than all right. I just wanted to give you some exciting news that I am sure you are going to love. Noelle told me last night that she scheduled her appointment with the office for her ultrasound. Do you want to guess when it is?" Angelina paused giving them time to answer.

"When is it?" The girls chimed in together.

Angelina continued, "She could not get in this week, so it's happening on Monday. Guess who'll be here to go with her?" They all heard the smile in Angelina's voice and she heard the shouts of cheers from the girls.

"Well", Genie said laughing, "you can certainly hear the excitement at this table. We will love being able to share that moment with her. You certainly made our day."

"She's going to be so surprised," Angelina continued. "Well, I can't stay on this phone. I have a busy day ahead and we certainly do not want Noelle to get suspicious. She thinks that she will be flying out on Wednesday to come home. I cannot wait for this all to play out. I love surprises. Okay, I have to go. You all have a great week. Drive safe and we'll see you when you get here."

With that, there was a round of good-byes as Genie hung up.

"Oh Mom, I can't wait. I wish that we could leave today." Nissa said.

"I know. Don't get any ideas, we can't." Genie emphasized the negatives. "Saturday morning will be here before you know it." She tried to encourage the girls.

Anaya frowned, "Not soon enough for me."

"Well let's get this day going then so that it rolls by as fast as possible. See you in the car in five minutes." Genie said as the girls were off on a run to do their last minute fixing and grab all of their stuff.

Secretly Genie thought the same thing that they did. This week could not be over fast enough for her either. Especially now they had the excitement of the ultrasound with Noelle, and the little one that her daughter carried, to anticipate. There was a definite feeling of relief. Then she stopped and marveled at how God had answered her concern about the ultra-sound. "You are so good God!" Genie smiled.

✱✱✱✱✱✱✱✱✱✱✱✱✱✱✱✱

Noelle rolled over in bed and gave up trying to go back to sleep. She was not ready to start her day yet. She really could have slept another hour. For the past 30 minutes, she had been pretending that she was asleep in hopes that it would happen; but…it did not. She had been sleeping so sound when the phone woke her. It was Nissa and she just wanted to say good morning and have a nice day. They had not talked very long, although it was long enough to cause her not to be able to find that sweet sleep.

While she lay in her bed, her mind began to wander again. The heavy questions that follow her were back. She could feel the weight of them almost as if they were pressing her down. Unfortunately, she could not hear the answers.

God what do I do? What do you have planned for this baby? Is this baby mine or is there another family just waiting with open arms? If that is Your plan, how do I do that? If I give my baby away, will I be able to live the rest of my life not knowing where he or she is? Will he play football? Will she someday

44

wear ballet shoes? I don't play an instrument; but there are genes from another person that I know nothing about involved here. Will the baby always remind me about that night? Help me Father. I need Your guidance.

Noelle's mind began to wander back to the night that changed her life forever. She thought about the excitement that she had experienced when the invitation came. She was going to a frat party as a freshman. She can still remember thinking that not everyone was so lucky. Her mind actually harbored the thought that the older guys must think that she had potential. She barely got through the week at school and she could not wait to get there. When she did, it was everything that she had imagined. People were everywhere. The music was loud. Everyone had a drink in his or her hand. Couples were dancing; and there were things going on in dark corners that, if she was honest with herself, were somewhat embarrassing. She tried not to look.

She remembered how friendly everyone was. They all seemed to want to know more about her. She didn't want to talk about who she was. She was there to forget about all that was going on in her life. Being there was her time to dull the nagging pain of her life with some drinks, meet some new people and enjoy college life. That night was her night and she planned to enjoy every minute.

What did she remember? She had walked into the kitchen where the drinks were. From that moment, everything became foggy. Noelle could remember thinking that the person that was mixing the drinks was nice. He had been telling jokes. Noelle can remember laughing with him, just silly stuff that did not really make any sense. Then everything began to spin. Dizzy. She was so dizzy. In her last cohesive thought, she wondered

45

would someone catch me if I fall. From that point on, there was nothing in her memory bank…just darkness.

Until the morning. She could remember opening her eyes just a little. They were so heavy it was difficult. The morning light was starting to come through the windows. The sun was not bright. In fact, there were moments when the sky was overcast. When the sun peaked through the clouds, it cast shadows on the wall that she was facing. Why am I having such a hard time waking up? She kept blinking her eyes trying to bring them into focus. The smells were nasty. She felt dirty. She turned her head and there he was with his naked back to her. Fear swallowed her. She could feel the bile in the back of her throat. Instantly she was awake. Minutes. It only took minutes for her to gather her clothes and be gone. Maybe it was less than minute. All she wanted was to be as far away from there as she could possibly get and as fast as she could go.

It was just one mistake. I certainly did not think any thing could happen to me. It was just a party. If I could just go back, I would have never gone there.

Now with a different perspective on life, and looking through the eyes of God, she knew it had all been so evil. Satan had deceived her; and back then, she did not even know it. He had done his job well. He came into her life and stole from her. He simply did one of his main jobs on this earth. He destroyed her life. At least her life as she knew it.

She began to pray.

"Why Lord? Why?"

"Remember your Creator in the days of your youth."

"I'm so sorry. Forgive me Father. I need Your loving guidance. I don't know what direction to turn.

46

I've messed everything up and I don't know how to make it right."

"Oh my Daughter, does My word not tell you that we wrestle not against flesh and blood, but against principalities, against powers, against the rulers of the darkness. Resist the devil and he will flee from you."

"What are you telling me Lord? I know that satan was directing my path and that is why I am in this situation. This is my fault. But how do I make everything right?"

"Oh my precious daughter, only I can make everything right again. Resist the devil and he will flee from you. Walk in my ways and I will direct your path."

Noelle thought for a minute while digesting all she felt the Lord was saying to her. Slowly it began to sink in. God was trying to warn her that satan was still trying to direct her. Satan was coming at her through the loneliness and despair she was allowing into her life now. That was not of God. She did not know much yet; but she did know that God was love, light, and goodness. She was dwelling in sorrow and sadness. She would never find God or His direction in the pits of despair.

"Is that what You are trying to tell me Father?"

"Never will I leave you; never will I forsake you."

"Oh Father thank you. I think that I am starting to understand. You want me to wait on You and You will direct my path. When I need the answers, You will give them to me. Right now, I just need to trust You. Thank you Father. Thank you."

Noelle knew beyond any doubt that God had just answered her prayers. He had just sent the peace that the Bible promises. She was going to try to live each day knowing that God is never late with an answer. Noelle determined that she was going to begin walking out her faith. This was an opportunity for her to trust that He

47

truly wanted what was best for her and the baby and that He would work towards that plan. Until then, she would wait for the Lord's answers and she would try to embrace each day as an opportunity to see Him at work in her life.

With that revelation received, she jumped out of bed and into the shower. This really *"was the day that the Lord had made."* She determined that she *"would rejoice and be glad in it."*

While she showered she thought on what would be the best way for her to stay out of the negative thoughts that so often weighed her down. Those thoughts were where the burdens started.

She realized that a joyful person would have an easier time thinking on God and His goodness.

Okay Noelle, how would you remain joyful? She thought to herself.

She thought only a moment and realized that she should be counting her blessings and not looking at her burdens. She began a sing song as she shampooed her hair. *If you're blessed, you have less stress! If you're blessed, you have less stress!*

She sang the words over and over, getting louder and louder each time.

If you're blessed, you have less stress. If you're blessed, you have less stress.

That song flowed into another and another...

Less stress, less mess. Less stress, less mess.

Happy life, no time for strife. Happy life, no time for strife.

Noelle found herself laughing uncontrollably as the water streamed down her face.

Father it really is true isn't it? Choosing joy is a decision that I make. I remember reading Father in your word that **'a merry heart doeth good like a**

48

medicine; but a broken spirit drieth the bones'. Well no more Father. I am choosing joy. I will laugh, even if I don't feel like laughing. Your word says that I can. I will count my blessings. First of all I have You. You are blessing me. I am thankful. You have provided a way for me. I have a home where people care about me. I have a family who loves me and You have provided a job where I can work diligently to meet the needs that I have. You are my ultimate keeper and all that I have is Yours. I will rejoice. I will call you Holy and You will call me Blessed. I will live under Your protective wing and all that You have promised for me will be mine. Thank you for Your Holy Spirit that gives me wisdom to understand all that has been revealed to me today. This day is Yours as are all of the others to come. I give You my life and the life of this child. I thank you for the answers that are to come and I wait in anticipation for Your blessings. I will be happy as I trust in You. AMEN and AMEN.

A new Noelle emerged from that shower. The old burdened Noelle had been washed away through the cleansing of His love.

Chapter Four

Psalm 96:4

For great is the Lord

and most worthy of praise;

He is to be feared above all Gods

BRAD AND EYAN WERE ALREADY AT THE KITCHEN bar when Angelina came down the stairs.

"Well just look at you," Eyan whistled. "Don't you look sassy?"

Angelina turned to look behind her pretending that she did not know that he was talking about her.

"What? Are you referring to, your aging mother?" She gave him a playful smile. Angelina loved the camaraderie that she shared with her two boys.

Brad jumped in, "You got a hot date that we don't know about?"

"Are you both worried that your momma might be choosing to spend her time with someone more mature than you boys?" She wrinkled her nose at them before pulling an egg casserole out of the refrigerator to warm up for breakfast.

"Whoa...lookie there Eyan! You're right she is a little sassy thing today." Brad said. "Maybe we're going to have to do something about that."

"Yah! Well that'll be the day when you two can out best your momma."

Eyan came around to the other side of the bar putting his coffee cup in the sink. Catching her with a quick kiss and saying, "Don't get me wrong...I like it when you're a little sassy. Nothing better than a spunky woman I say. I also say just coffee for me, no eggs today. I have a breakfast date with the college group from church. Some of us are meeting for a morning Bible study. I'm off. You guys have a great day and I'll see you both tonight," he said as he headed for the door.

Just as he did, he caught Noelle coming down the

stairs to join the group for breakfast.

"Gee whiz! All these good-looking women and I'm heading out the door. Something's wrong with my timing."

Noelle giggled as she raised her hand and wiggled her fingers good-bye at Eyan.

Angelina flicked her hand towel at him and said, "You best be behaving, or I'll take a broom to you."

"Yes Momma." He said as he closed the door leaving only the image of the smirk on his face behind.

"Good morning." Brad smiled at Noelle as she took the stool beside him.

"Good morning to you." She answered back.

Angelina was getting plates of egg casserole with lots of bubbling cheese ready for the both of them. On the side was some turkey ham fried nice and toasty brown and a few slices of grilled pineapple. "Milk or juice?" She asked them.

"Milk, please." They both answered at the same time.

Looking at each other, they smiled.

After her time spent with the Lord this morning, Noelle felt like every thing was a reason to smile. Life was just lighter. She was going to have a great day.

Handing their breakfast plates to each of them, Angelina sat down with her plate of food on a stool across from Brad and Noelle. She looked at Noelle and then looked again. Taking a closer look she asked, "Something is changed about you? You're sporting a different look from last night."

"I'm a new creation, old things have passed away. The Lord has offered me a new start and I am taking Him up on His offer. No more is satan going to manipulate me into worrying about tomorrow. God holds it in His hands anyway, right? I am just going to press forward, wait, and see what the Lord has in store for the baby and me. He knows best. Why should I worry about the things that I don't know, especially if He already has the answers? I'll just wait on Him to direct my path." Noelle finished as she took a bite of the eggs. "By the way…these eggs are delicious!"

Brad and Angelina were speechless as they stared at Noelle.

"Well…chalk one up for God. I am glad to see the change. I was getting tired just watching you struggle with the burdens that you were carrying. God does not want us to carry a heavy load. He has a better way. Praise Him! His mercies are new every day. He tells us in his word that the very hairs on our head are numbered. God not only knows how many hairs you have, He has given each one of them a number. That is amazing. If He's that concerned about your hairs, you have to know that he cares even more about everything that's going on in your life today and everyday." Angelina said.

"Oh His goodness! Listen to the scripture for the day." Angelina began to read from the Day-by-Day Devotional Calendar that she kept on the snack bar.

Because of the Lord's great love, we are not consumed, for his compassions never fail. They are new every morning; great is Your faithfulness.
Lamentations 3:22-23

"That…His children, is how good our God is! If that does not show us how He masterminds every little detail of our lives, nothing will. He is a recovery specialist. What happened to you was totally satan at work; but satan can't win in your life as long as you apply the cross of Jesus Christ. When you do that, you connect with God and His power will take over in your life. The old is gone and the new has come." Angelina set the devotional aside with a look on her face that said she was quite excited about her God. You could see that she loved to share His Word.

"You know what I think Miss Smith?" Brad tilted his head as he smiled at Noelle.

"I don't know…what do you think Mr. Conroy?" Noelle followed his teasing lead.

"Two things; one…I'm reminded that God says you're worth more than a sparrow and two…I think that revelations like the one you've experienced today deserves to be celebrated. Don't you Mom?"

"What a great idea. Noelle has been working too hard everyday. What do you have in mind?" Angelina continued her discussion with her son as if Noelle was not sitting right there in their midst.

"I'm thinking that I'll pick her up at the restaurant around 6:00 p.m. and take her into Indy for a movie and supper. What do you say Miss Noelle?"

"I say that's a lovely offer; but I can't leave your mom hanging during the evening meal. She'd be short a server."

"Nonsense! I'll be just fine. I will simply work the floor instead of floating around. You two go and have a great time." Angelina insisted.

"No…it's impossible." Noelle continued as if Angelina hadn't just tried to make the decision for her, "Plus, I'll miss four hours of tips. That is proving to be a lot of money and I am going to have big expenses soon. I need to make all of the money that I can right now. Who knows what may be around the corner. I have to be ready for whatever God has in store for me. And let's not forget that I am going to be gone most of next week too." Noelle said.

"Honey, you can't work twelve hours every day. You will be so tired. That is not good for the baby or you.

I have been worrying daily about the hours that you are working. Now, I insist that you go with Brad and have a good time tonight. We will be fine at the restaurant. I love that you are so conscientious of others…but not tonight. You are going, you are not going to worry about what is happening at the restaurant and that is an order. Just enjoy." Angelina finished with the look on her face that said that was that and there would be no arguing.

"Okay it's settled. I'll be there at 6:00 sharp and we'll eat a late supper after a movie." Brad ended as he picked up his empty plate, rinsed it and put it in the dishwasher.

Noelle smiled, "Well I guess that I've been over ruled. A movie and dinner it is. So…," she shrugged, "I guess I'll be ready at 6:00. Sharp."

"Great. Wow...getting a date never used to be this hard. I must need to brush up on my skills. They must be getting rusty." Brad kissed his mother on the check on his way by.

"See you girls tonight," he said as he headed for the door. On the way by Noelle, he ruffled her hair. She jumped as if she had been shocked and he was sure that he could almost feel the electric jolt through his hand.

Someday she is going to rock my world. He was smiling as he walked out the door.

Noelle and Angelina sat quietly eating their breakfast deep in thought. It was a comfortable quiet. The rest of their day would be busy and loud.

As she was finishing her breakfast, Angelina's mind was mulling over what she had just seen in her son's face. Again, trusting, she threw up a silent prayer, *Father, protect my son and lead him where you want him to go.*

"Angelina, my daughter, he is my son too."

Angelina knew she was worrying about him unnecessarily. She knew that Brad belonged to the Lord and that God was not going to take him anywhere that would bring chaos into his life. God was a God of order, not a God of chaos.

✶✶✶✶✶✶✶✶✶✶✶✶✶✶✶✶

So many thoughts were running through Brad's mind as he was driving to school. All of them intertwined with Noelle. He was already excited about spending time with her again. There had not been much time for the two of them to talk since she had gotten back. She seemed to spend every minute that she could at the restaurant. Even when his mother was not there, there were days that she went in early or stayed late. This morning's conversation shed some light on the long hours. The reality dawned on Brad. She must be worrying about money and now that makes perfect sense. The responsibility that she's facing is huge. The question facing her is whether she is going to keep the baby.

Brad would love to have that conversation with her; but he was not sure how to ask those questions. Would she even want to discuss that with him? If the Lord plans to give Noelle to me as a life mate, where do I fit in the

future of this child? Either way, her decision will affect me. If she chooses to keep the baby, I will be getting a package deal. An insty mix family, if you will. If she gives the baby up for adoption, then I will have to support her and deal with the emotional consequences that will come with knowing that she has a child that she carried for nine months inside of her; a child that she

56

does not know. He was not sure which would be harder for her or for him.

Brad did the only thing that made sense when faced with a major decision; he went to prayer.

"Father, I'm sure that I haven't heard you wrong. I think that you have brought Noelle here to be my life long partner and I can be patient until You say the time is right for that to happen. How do I support her through this though? Do You want her to keep the baby? Is she struggling with that decision now? Could I help her someway? Show me Your will for our lives. Are You not only calling me to be a husband, but also a father? What if I'm not good enough for that job? That is not something that I can fail at with another person's life hanging in the balance."

"Love covers all that we don't know my Son."

"But Father, do I have enough love to make this child my own?"

"I have enough love to make this child my own. You have me. I created this child in my image. I make no mistakes. By my breath the body lives. I had a plan and purpose for this child before the beginning of time. Trust me, my son, trust me."

"Thank you Father. I will trust You."

A peace came over Brad and he knew that everything was going to be okay. Somehow, he did plan to find a way to talk to Noelle about the baby. He did not know how he was going to do it; but he wanted her to know that she was not alone. He knew that God was putting them together as a family. He did not know how that looked yet. He had another year of school. There was the farm and his mom, not to mention his mom's restaurant. Yes, there were so many decisions that would have to work out.

Then Brad laughed to himself. Here he was putting a plan together to start a family and working through all of the ABC's of what that looked like and he hadn't even talked to the girl. That was definitely a 'cart before the horse moment'. First things first. He thought to himself.

Brad began to play out the other side of the scenario; he did not want Noelle deciding to be a mother based on what he wanted to happen. Being a mother had to be her decision...not his. He wanted to have a family with a woman who was sold out on nurturing and loving with everything in her being.

If Brad was going to be honest with himself, Noelle was new to living a life based on what God wanted and not on what she wanted. This pregnancy had not started very well. It would be easy to see anger and bitterness taking root. That thought made Brad think about a bulletin board that he had seen. It said, "Anger is just the letter "D" away from being danger." God had a lot of work to do yet for all of this to come together.

Then he thought about how quickly life can turn around when God is in control. Look at the story of Joseph in Genesis. His brothers sell him into slavery because of jealousy. He ends up in the house of Potiphar, one of Pharaoh's officials. Potiphar sees that Joseph has found favor in the eyes of the Lord and that he prospers. He gives him charge of all that he owns. Potiphar's wife makes advances towards Joseph and even though Joseph does the right thing, the wife makes up lies about him trying to seduce her. Joseph's master believes his wife and puts Joseph in prison. Even in prison, he was in charge of all that happened there. He is in prison with some of the King's officials and he interprets their dreams. His interpretations come true. Two full years later, the King has a dream; they tell him that Joseph can interpret the dream. They bring Joseph. He interprets the dream and

58

he finds favor in the eyes of Pharaoh. Within a day, God has brought him out of prison and into the King's service where he was dressed in fine robes, given the King's signet ring, a gold chain around his neck and a chariot to ride in. Joseph becomes the King's second-in-command and in charge of all of Egypt. That is how fast God can move when He decides to. Brad decided to rest in God's care and see where He was going to take all of this.

However, he was hoping that tonight they could talk some and Brad could get a feel for where her heart was heading. God was doing a work. He saw that in Noelle this morning. Noelle's spirit had taken a leap in the right direction. She was learning to trust; not something that you learn over night, and not always easily grasped. Sometimes it is just a definite decision that you make. You decide that you are going to trust and then you just walk that out. That was what Brad was going to do starting right now. Let God be God and follow where He leads.

With that decided, Brad was pulling into the campus parking lot. Today was going to be a great day. He could already feel it. There was crispness to the air as he jumped out of the truck. Every day there were more and more signs of new life; flowers were popping up and leaves that gracefully unfurled themselves on the branches of trees that had stood naked all winter. Brad loved spring. Everything was so fresh and clean. It made you realize that all was right in the world, at least in Brad's world.

Chapter Five

Psalm 96:5

For all the gods of the nations

are idols,

But the Lord made the heavens

NGELINA AND NOELLE TALKED AS THEY DROVE
to the restaurant. When they got there the
breakfast crowd was well under way. Noelle was feeling so much guilt about leaving Angelina short handed
later during the dinner shift that she was determined to
work twice as hard as she normally would. And she
did. When there were no customers to wait on, she was
preparing what she could for the evening meals. As
Noelle was doing that, Angelina went into the kitchen to
get deserts going for the evening meals. The kitchen had
a separate room where everything was set up to make the
pies and other deserts. That way she would be out of the
bustle of the chef in the kitchen.

Angelina actually loved to work in this room.
She could hear the chatter of her staff and feel the energy
that was buzzing around in there; yet in this room, off
by herself there was a calm that engulfed her. She loved
mixing the pastry and feeling the dough in her hands.
Making pies for her was more of an art than anything
else that she did. She felt she was creating and each one
was a different masterpiece. Her pies were as much a
decoration as they were a perfect taste to melt in your
mouth. Her mixing room was equipped with all of the
niceties that made the job go so smoothly. It did not
take long before she had an assembly line of piecrusts
just waiting for the fillings that were going to complete
them. Through the holiday seasons, it had been pecan
and pumpkin that were the pies of choice. As the world
outside brightened with the hope of spring, people chose
more fruit pies and lighter custards. Before she knew
it, she would have fresh berries coming in from her farm

and the farmer's market. Until then she would have to work with what she had. There was always a high demand for the creams and of course the "All American" apple pie. However, something told her today was a cake day, so to serve with the pies she made a triple layer, red velvet fudge with a cherry pie filling mixed in. Just one, first come…first served.

That done, she started in on the homemade breads and rolls. Angelina's desserts were another reason that her customers always came back. As her servers were in and out of the swinging doors to the kitchen, those dining could catch the smell of breads baking in the ovens. Especially on a day like today, with a little bit of chill in the air, the homemade soups at lunch with a fresh, out of the oven roll would hit the spot. Then they would top it off with a yummy dessert and be on their way, eager to come back another day.

Angelina knew that her location was perfect. She was close enough to all of the businesses that she would catch those who wanted to escape for that hour. Yet she was casual enough that those who get dirty on their jobs still felt comfortable stopping in for that warm lunch before they were back on duty.

The restaurant had been an answer to her prayers. She had been so lost when Terran, the boys' dad, had died so suddenly. She loved being a mom; but that left her with too much time in the day by herself. She had always done a lot of volunteer work and still did. However, Angelina knew that she had to jump in with both feet into something, which would not only support her but also fill the empty, gapping hole that Terran's death had left in her life.

The boys and she had lost him so suddenly; there had been no way to see the life change coming. One

62

day He was with them alive and vibrant and the next he was there on the barn floor lifeless and gone from them. There were so many areas of struggle for her when it happened. First, he had died by himself. She was not there holding him and telling him that she loved him. The medical examiner told her repeatedly that he had died instantly. One second he was here and the next he was with the Heavenly Father. Her church family was so supportive during her grieving. They reminded her regularly that as a couple they had said all of the right words every day. They spoke of love daily, the love they had for the boys and the love that they had for each other. When she was not stuck in her grief, she knew that. Second, they were best friends. They spent every day together. Farming drew them closer together. They loved to work side-by-side daily. If it was fieldwork, she was there. In the barn, you would find her by his side. When he left, she was lost and lonely. The grief would close in on her and it was debilitating. Oh she had the boys to care for and they needed her more than ever. During the day when they were at school, she would climb back into bed and cry her day away. She grabbed hold of enough energy to meet their physical needs; and she loved them. To this day she can still remember the feeling of no more and no less. She clung to her boys and to her God that sustained her.

Then one day she heard a pastor talking about walking through the problem to get to the provision. He was saying that the greater the promises of God the greater the problems. To this day she can still hear him say, "How you react to the problem determines how long you stay in the problem. The Hand of God is trying to show us what is in us." His teaching was saying that the problem that is the hardest for you to stand up under is the one where God will teach you the most. His question, "How do you act in the fire?"

She picked up her Bible and began to study everyday. Sometimes she did it through tears. She forced herself to rejoice even when her heart was breaking. Music is such a soothing vessel of healing. God's music played everyday. It resounded through her house. Even when she did not have it in her to sing, the music touched spots in her soul.

I Peter 4:19 became, what she called her "grab hold of verse". It says,

So then, those who suffer according to God's will should commit themselves to their faithful Creator and continue to do good.

Angelina got to a spot where she realized that if she wanted out of the problem of sorrow, she had to take authority over the pain. She realized through His word that she would stay in the problem until she wanted to solve it. She knew that only with God's help could she move forward. She also understood that moving forward did not mean that she had to forget the past; she just could not look back at the past as if it was better than the future. Their life together had been amazing. She had been a blessed woman; a wonderful man had loved her. Terran had taught her how to be strong and stand through adversity. Now she had to make a decision to walk into the future sure that God would be right by her side. His promises told her that He would comfort her, He would lift her up and carry her on those hard days, and He would love her with a love that would surrender His life for her.

Angelina decided she needed a plan. She would do what God had called her to do, serve. That was what she loved doing anyway. So, she began to build a future following the passion of her heart. She took part of the money from Terran's insurance policy, bought this old building, and started remodeling it into the perfect restaurant. It was a huge risk that paid off.

Thank goodness, her husband had planned for an emergency and had taken care of his family. It allowed Angelina to build a new life without her mate; one that fulfilled her need to serve and allowed her a direction for new dreams.

This had certainly not been what she would have chosen. Terran had been the love of her life. She never planned to have to build a new life with out the love of the man who stood by her no matter what. She was just continuing life after it changed directions on her. It was proving to be a fulfilling life; one that she would look back on with fondness when that day came. People would say to her, "You are young. You will find love again." Yet, in her heart of hearts, she knew that she had loved above and beyond. Love like the one they had shared was rare. She defined herself through the eyes of Jesus and didn't feel the need, at least during this place in her life, to consider loving that passionately again. She was finding true contentment in raising her boys and the work at the restaurant. She was serving and for now, that was enough.

Angelina came out of her mental wandering as she finished the breads and was placing them into the ovens. She had spent enough time daydreaming for today. It was time to make sure that everything was ready for the lunchtime diners.

On her way out of the kitchen, Angelina threw up a quick prayer. *"Thank you God for all that you have given to me and my family. We love You Lord. Bring me the lost and hurting so that I can show them what a lov-*

*ing God You are. It is Your day Lord. Help me to use it
for Your Kingdom's gain. Please stretch forth the Hand
of God. Instruct Your Angels to watch over us and show
us Your favor. Amen."*

That said, she walked into the dining room only to
find out that Noelle and the others had everything ready
to go and were grabbing a quick bite before the crowds
hit. She grabbed a small salad, sat down with them, and
enjoyed the good time that her workers shared.

✶✶✶✶✶✶✶✶✶✶✶✶✶✶✶✶

Michelle and Noelle had been the first to sit
down and grab something to eat. It had not been that
long since they had eaten that wonderful breakfast that
Angelina had ready this morning. However, already her
stomach was grumbling at her. She had begun to realize
that she needed to keep something in her stomach at all
times to keep it happy. She did not like the feeling when
it was not happy. She tried to nibble a little something
every couple of hours. This day she had jumped into
work as soon as they had arrived at the restaurant and
now it was saying, "eat…now…eat." So…she did.

Michelle already had a large serving of potato
salad and some olives.

"How do you stay so little? You eat the worst
diet of anyone that I know. I would weigh 200 lbs. if I
ate all of the fat and starch that you eat." Noelle laughed.

"I have an eating disorder. I just eat and it's all
out of order. So do not 'dis' me!" Michelle tried to give
her a gangster look, as she shook her finger at Noelle, but
failed miserably. Both girls began to laugh and could not
stop once they got going.

Finally pulling herself together Michelle looked

at Noelle and said, "You know…there's something different about you today. You're so uptight. What's up with that?"

"Sometime we'll need to have a long talk; but for right now I'll just say that I've been struggling with a huge load and this morning I just decided to let God carry it instead. It was just getting too heavy and burdensome." Noelle finished.

Michelle smiled, "I was just praying about you last night. It was so evident that you have a problem that is weighing on you. I wanted to help and I decided that we are going to have to get together. I want to share with you what my Savior has done for me so that I did not have to live a miserable life. So…I am up for a meeting of the minds. Let's do it soon."

"That sounds good to me. However, it cannot be tonight. I was over ruled this morning at breakfast and I'm being picked up by Brad at 6:00 today for a movie and supper out." Noelle shrugged as she took a bite of her salad.

"Don't act like that'll be such a struggle. Do you know that Brad is the most sought after single person around this town and as far as that goes, surrounding towns? Every girl who knows him wants to be the one that he chooses. He is the most real deal going. What an awesome guy." Michelle gave that wishful look to Noelle. "I wish he was picking me up. I'd be jumping for joy."

"Oh I know what a great guy he is. Tonight is not anything like that though. He's just being nice." Noelle wanted to tell Michelle that Brad did not need everything that came with her. He certainly did not need to yoke himself to a single mom with an illegitimate baby, or a girl who was going to live the rest of her life knowing

67

that she had a baby that she would never know. He did not have to deal with a load of regrets that could plague someone in her situation. No Brad would attach himself to someone who was perfect; just like him."

I see you white as snow. Your sin is gone, as far as the east is from the west.

Noelle recognized the quiet reminder from her loving father and smiled.

"Well whatever tonight is," Michelle said, "I would enjoy every minute and hope for more."

With that, the rest of the crew joined them and shortly even Angelina sat down for a quick lunch. The conversations became lighter and they all had a few minutes of silliness that released the stress of the breakfast rush and helped them get ready for the lunch crowd. Angelina had discovered years ago that laughter kept her work family happier and happier servers made for happier customers. So…they laughed and she enjoyed every minute of their time together.

Noelle's mind did want to drift back to the words from Michelle about Brad, and even though she knew that she should not do it, there was an anticipation that was building.

✻✻✻✻✻✻✻✻✻✻✻✻✻✻✻✻

Brad's morning classes had gone surprisingly quick, he was on his way home to finish a few chores; then a shower, and he would be on his way to pick up Noelle.

He was certainly eager and there was this churning in the pit of his stomach. All morning he had been thinking about the conversation that he felt God was pushing him into. It just seemed right. What if Noelle was not ready to hear what he was about to offer, He wondered. She did not even know him and he did not know what she was thinking about the baby. Then maybe tonight was the night to have that talk. After all, they did not get much time together to have the kind of talks that would give him the answers to the questions that he wanted to ask.

"Lord I think that I'm going in the direction that You want me to go; if that's true then will You please pave the way for me. I mean, what if Noelle is not ready to hear any of this. I don't want to scare her away or put any undue pressure on her. What if she ..."

"Don't be a doubting Thomas my son. Go where I send you. I would never lead you in the wrong direction. My sheep hear my voice and they know it. You know it. I will be with you every step of the way. I love you my son."

Instantly there was peace and Brad knew that all was going to be okay. Whatever Noelle said, he would be obedient to the Lord.

At 5:50, Angelina came to Noelle while she was getting a salad ready for the table that she was waiting on and said, "Let me take over for you now so that you can get ready for Brad."

Noelle looked at her and started to protest. They were so busy tonight that she was feeling terribly guilty leaving in the start of what was looking to be an exceptional rush hour. "Angelina I can't leave you short a person, this crowd is really ramping up to be a long night. You are going to need me. Your staff are going to have to work to hard to cover my spot."

"Nonsense, don't even start that with me. I have been running this restaurant for years. You're going to go and have a great time with my son...That's an order!" She was not going to hear any objection.

Angelina took the salad bowl and fluffed her hand in the air at Noelle, leaving her nothing more to do than to go. She had brought a dress and jacket to slip into so that she did not have to wear the clothes that she had worked in all day. She was glad to have a few minutes to freshen up. This would be the first time that Brad would see her in something other than her casual clothes. She could not help but wonder what he would think about how she looked.

At exactly 6:00 p.m., Brad, never late, walked into the restaurant. Noelle was walking towards the front desk right on time.

"Wow! You look great." Brad said with a smile that caused Noelle's stomach to do a little flutter.

"Thank you. You...are very punctual. I have to say that I feel a little guilty leaving your mom working so hard. This'll be a long day for her."

"If Mom hadn't wanted you to go, she would have said that tonight wasn't a good night. Believe me, I know my mom well enough to know that she speaks her mind. Everything is fine. Let's go and have a great time. As good as you look; maybe we should leave Mom the truck and take the SUV." Brad paused serious in thought.

"Now you are being silly. The truck is fine. In fact, I like riding in the truck. That big truck makes me feel like we're in charge of the road." Noelle giggled.

With that, Brad shook his head smiling and said, "Well in that case, let's go boss." He hoped that she would never cease to surprise him. As they got to the truck, Brad took extra care helping Noelle into the seat. Then strapping her seat belt, he shut the door. As Brad walked around the front of the truck, Noelle marveled at the little things that he did that made her feel so special. He jumped into the truck and they were off.

It took them a little more than an hour to drive into Indianapolis from the restaurant. Brad explained that he had checked out the movies and they were in-between start times. He had made reservations for them to have dinner first, if that was okay with her.

"It's actually perfect. I haven't eaten since right before the lunch crowd and I'm starving." Noelle answered.

"Perfect."

The restaurant was beautiful. It was very quaint and quiet. They seated them in the front so that she could see all of the white lights that were still up and glowing all around the street. It was fun to watch the bustle of the people as they rushed from storefront to storefront. Who couldn't love this time of the year? The promise of spring was right around the corner. Everything was coming to life. Green was such a clean color replacing the dingy color of winter as it passed away. Snow covers such a muddy look before the new life comes.

Noelle thought about that in relation to her situation. There had been ugliness covering the beauty that God had just waited to burst forth in her life. He was the new life and through Him, she was beginning to feel that new life that she was birthing day by day. Angelina and Brad had planted the seed and God's Word was feeding and watering it. She loved feeling it grow in her life. All around her new life was happening. In her life, it was happening too.

The host asked for their drink orders and Noelle

said that she would like water with lemon. Brad ordered black coffee with water on the side.

"Brad, I do want to say thank you for this night. It is lovely. I forgot how nice it is to get away and just be… with no time constraints or pressures. I am going to enjoy the time that is just you and me. I have been here three months and we have barely had time to sit and have a real conversation. This is so nice. I really appreciate that you suggested this."

"I have to confess. I think this night is more for me than for you. I have wanted to whisk you away for some time. You keep yourself so busy that the time just never seemed to happen. I want more of this."

His admission surprised Noelle. Out of her mouth slipped, "Why?"

Brad paused as he looked at her. After the shock of her question settled in, laughing he realized that she did not have a clue that he had feelings for her. He answered, "Why not?"

Now it was Noelle's turn to be surprised. "I'm not in the best of situations. There aren't many men who would want to beat down my door to walk into this mess."

"I'm not like most men Noelle." Brad answered.

Noelle really stopped to look at Brad. She was surprised to see that the expression on his face was very serious. She was speechless. Her arms began to tingle and she could feel a quickening in the rhythm of her heart.

"Noelle, what are you thinking about the baby? Is it okay if I ask that? I don't want you to think that I'm prying."

The question took Noelle by surprise. "What do you mean?"

"Well, I'm thinking that you're five months along, more than half way. You must think about what is going to happen in the next four months. You are definitely going to have a baby. Have you made any decisions? Do you think about keeping the baby or is your plan to give the baby up for adoption?" Brad slowed as he asked the last questions. He wanted time for them to register.

Noelle took a deep breath. "I do think about it. I was worrying about it so much that my mind was always in turmoil, until this morning. Then I turned it over to God. I felt reassured that He was working it all out. I don't know how. I just realized that if He always has a plan and purpose for each of us, then that means for my baby too. I wish that everything were different. If it were, I would keep my baby and try to be the best mother to my child. Then I begin to wonder, am I being unfair to the baby. This baby deserves two parents who will love and nurture him or her. I'm sure there is a family out there just waiting with empty arms. They could give my baby so much more than I could by myself. Then again, I want to be selfish. I don't want to spend a life time wondering what my child's life is like. The biggest question becomes this, would this baby be a constant reminder of the ugliness of that night. Can I get past that?"

Noelle paused as if she were considering all of the questions ever so carefully.

"So…for now I don't have the answers. I only know that God has been guiding my steps ever since I ran away. I don't think that He is going to stop now. So I'll wait on Him."

Brad had his answer. Noelle would want to keep her baby. She would want to be a mother to her child and build a family. As for the start of this baby, Brad was sure that as Noelle grew in the love of the Lord, He would heal the wounds from that night for her.

He smiled at Noelle and said, "You're doing the most important thing that you can. You are letting God be in control. He will not steer you wrong. I know that you are right. He does have a plan. God is never late. He's working it all out."

"Good. I cannot wait to see what wonderful plans He has. He is a God of abundance, right. Whatever He's planning has got to be better than I can even imagine." Noelle finished and began to study the menu.

"You can bet that's true. I will agree that you cannot even imagine." Brad chuckled to himself, "Now what looks good?"

On that note, Brad ended that conversation and focused on enjoying the rest of the evening. His heart was soaring. He had his answer and he knew where God was going. Now all that he had to do was wait on God and His timing. Everything else would work itself out.

Chapter Six

Psalm 96:6

Splendor and majesty are before Him;

Strength and glory are in His sanctuary

NOELLE WOKE AND STRETCHED. JOY WAS FLOOD-ing through her spirit. It felt good and seemed like it had been a long time since she could remember feeling sparks of happiness. She laid her hand on her tummy and as she rubbed it soothingly she said, "Baby, I want you to know I love you. Even if I don't get to be your mommy everyday of your life, I will always be your first mommy. And no one will ever love you as much as I always will."

Saying those words brought tears to her eyes. She wondered if the baby could feel the love that she was trying to send. As the baby grew, more and more she wanted to be a part of his or her life. Less and less, she thought about what had happened to her that night. God was taking her mess and making all things new. After all, that was what He promised. ***He hath sent me to heal the brokenhearted, to preach deliverance to the captives. Luke 4:18.*** Noelle understood that broken feeling. The last year of her life had been full of broken. Then she found the love of a Savior and everything changed. No longer did she have to live in the pit of despair. There were options in her life and choices that she could make that were life changing. She was going to believe by faith that everything was going to be okay in the end. She had just read Hebrews 11. She was starting to understand a little more about faith. As she read, "By faith Abraham, when God tested him, offered Isaac; By faith Isaac blessed; By faith Jacob, when he was dying; By faith Joseph, when his end was near…" She was realizing that faith is an action. Noelle decided that faith requires you to do something. And in that movement towards God, you are blessed.

After thinking on this and praying, Noelle decided that from this moment on, she was going to walk by faith through this pregnancy. She was going to trust that God had a wonderful plan and that He was in charge. She was going to wait for Him to reveal His "good and perfect plan."

She had read in ***Romans 8: 37-39 "…we are more than conquerors through Him who loved us. For I am persuaded that neither death nor life, nor angels nor principalities nor powers, nor things present nor things to come, nor height nor depth, nor any other created thing, shall be able to separate us from the love of God which is in Christ Jesus our Lord."***

When she had studied that verse in her Bible the footnote talked about Paul, who had written Romans. He wanted to show that suffering does not separate believers from Christ but actually carries them along toward their ultimate goal. She found out suffering has always been part of the experience of God's people. The verses are saying that it is impossible to beyond God's love reach. When it talks about 'Him who loved us' it is actually referring to Christ's death on the cross.

For Noelle it always came back to what He did for her. The very thought that there was a man who did not even know her; yet knew every intimate detail of her and loved her, brought her such joy. That this mortal man, yet still the Son of God, was willing to carry that cross, after the beating that He took, all the way up that hill and then climb onto that cross all by himself. No man put Him there. He chose to be a willing sacrifice for all of humanity. Through His words in the Bible, she had grasped how personal His death had been for her… and her baby. Noelle understood that in the good times and the bad times, the God of creation was always with her and always loving her.

She started her day by praying and thanking Him for all He had done for her already. She prayed for her family and the family that had taken her in and shown her the true love of the Lord. She asked blessings on all of them. Then in mid prayer, she felt God drop a thought into her spirit.

"What about the father of the baby? Will you ask Me to bless him also?"

She was shocked. Noelle knew the answer that God was waiting for…but how could He really expect her to do it? Could she pray for the boy that had changed her life so drastically? Then she thought, "By faith…"

"Lord, I'm going to need Your help to do this. Here goes. Father, bless the boy that raped me. Change his life. Put someone in his path that will teach him who You are. Make him a new creation. In Jesus Name. Amen"

Noelle decided to start with addressing the rape. She was not at a place that would allow her to associate him with the life of her child.

"Father, I hope that pleases You. It is the best that I can do for now. I am stepping out in faith and trusting that You will make it easier every time that I say it. Thank you for guiding me in all righteousness even when I do not want to go there willingly. I love you God."

On that note, Noelle rolled out of bed and hurried to the shower. It was a great way to start her day, talking to the Father. It made everything seem as if it was in balance. Before she found God, who was just waiting for her to come to Him, there was no balance in her life anywhere. Every area seemed to be upside down. She liked this new revelation. It was more than peace. She truly was a new creation. When she thought about the old her, it was with the acknowledgement that the old Noelle was no more. She was gone. Never to be resurrected again. The old Noelle was full of anger and bitterness. That had only led to strife and turmoil in her life. Now she was eager to see the joy that God was going to bring. She liked thinking that she was fresh everyday. That was how she felt. She thought to herself, I wonder what people do who never find the love of the Lord. How do they do the day to day?

Instantly, she thought about her earthly father. What does he do or feel everyday? Is there sadness and remorse in his life? Does he look back and wonder… what if?

As the shower water ran over her hair, Noelle could begin to feel the tugging of the old feelings wanting to well up inside of her. Just the thoughts of the father that had broken her heart into so many pieces caused an instant sinking in her spirit. Recognizing what was happening, she said, "No. Get lost satan. You have no control here. You are not welcome. I know what you are trying to do. You want to steal my joy. Well you cannot. I will not let you. I have found the answers and they do not have anything to do with you. You tried to destroy my baby and me. Not now. No more. Be gone from my thoughts." Noelle was proud of herself for being aware enough to see the attack that satan was throwing her way. She was thankful for the "discerning spirit" that she just recognized. In fact, she was going to take it one-step farther by faith…

"Father, would you also bless my dad, while you're spreading your blessings around today? You can love him best of all. I am going to put him in Your hands today and forever. In fact, I am thinking about

80

*forgiving him. Can you help that feel like a normal thing
for me to do? Bless my mom and sisters too. Maybe You
could bring them to the point of feeling normal about
forgiving dad too while You're at it. Thanks God. I love
You again!"*

She had learned that people limit God, not
acknowledging what He can do through them. If she
was going to surrender, she wanted to give up every
doubt and fear. She wanted that complete understanding
of what He could do in her life, while she was learning to
surrender her desires and find Him. She knew that God
had a plan and a purpose for her and her baby. Now she
just needed to wait on Him for the answers.

With that, Noelle's thoughts turned to last night
with Brad. It had been wonderful. The meal that they
ate was close to Angelina's meals. However, as far as
Noelle was concerned, no one could do it the way that
Angelina did it. Better yet was the time that Brad and
she had spent talking and laughing. Noelle could always
find something humorous when she was with Brad. He
just brought out the best in everything; including her.

After dinner, they had decided not to go to a
movie. She was glad. They just went for a walk in downtown Indianapolis. They browsed little quaint shops and
talked as they watched the bustle of people everywhere.
The night was perfect. The air had that clean, spring feel
to it. The kind of air that you can only smell after the
long winter has gone and the promise of new life was
everywhere. They were having a light conversation,
when Noelle felt Brad take her hand and gently lead her
across the street. The best part was that he did not let go.

Noelle let her mind roam back to that moment.
She could feel the warmth of his large hand as it cradled
her smaller hand. She marveled at the contrast between

81

the hard calluses from his farm work to the possessive yet gentle feel of his fingers as they intertwined themselves between her fingers. She liked the feel of that. It was protecting; but not smothering. She could have pulled away if she had wanted. He was not holding so hard that she felt controlled. No, it was almost a feeling of support. Just enough pressure to let her know that, if she needed him, he was there. Yet, she could be free and she sensed that he would encourage her to run ahead and explore life. The feeling gave her confidence. For the first time in her life, she considered the intimacy of holding hands. She liked it...She liked having Brad hold her hand very much, maybe too much for her situation.

They passed a small shop with merchandise set up outside. As they stopped to browse, a man came toward them and said, "You should buy your pretty lady a beautiful scarf to match her beautiful face." Noelle laughed; but Brad said, "You are absolutely right. I think that I should buy my pretty lady a beautiful scarf."

Had Noelle read the tone in his voice wrong when it seemed that he had emphasized 'my' pretty lady?

The vendor offered Brad a loud, variegated orange scarf with tassels on the ends. Brad reached for a fine crocheted cream-colored scarf. "I think this looks more like a scarf for a beautiful lady."

After paying for it, Brad turned and holding the scarf up asked, "May I?"

Looking into his eyes, Noelle answered softly, "please."

Brad draped the scarf around Noelle's shoulders tying it gently in a knot that hung at the perfect length. Looking at his choice, he smiled and lightly kissed the top of her head. He tenderly allowed his lips to linger for a moment in time.

82

The merchant laughed, "A fine choice, but I think that I could have done a better job of the kiss."

"Oh, no sir." Brad answered back. "A lady is like fine china. She has to be treated with tenderness." Brad's eyes never left hers as he answered the man back. He seemed to be looking straight into her soul. Noelle was sure that at that exact moment her heart temporarily stopped beating.

Thanking the man for suggesting the scarf, they walked away listening to the man's laughter as he said to himself, "What about this younger generation?" Brad again took hold of Noelle's hand and they continued walking.

It took Noelle a few minutes to find her voice. "Thank you for the scarf; and for the things that you said. You make me feel like a treasure."

"That is exactly what God created you to be, a precious treasure. Don't ever think differently. If you ever need me to remind you, just say so."

"Okay." She smiled at him before looking away. She had to acknowledge that funny feeling in the pit of her stomach again. What was going on? Was she reading more into Brad's kindness?

These were great thoughts to contemplate first thing in the morning. As she stood in the shower, a ealization came over her. Brad holding her hand was intentional. He was saying to those that they passed, "We're a couple." The thought paused her completely. She began to think about the rest of the night. They had stopped for dessert at a quiet coffee shop they past. The aroma of the freshly baked cookies drew them in. He had held her chair as she sat down. She watched as he went to the counter and waited to get a variety of cookies and two glasses of milk. He caught her studying him, he

83

winked at her and she blushed.

Coming back with his hands full, their hands brushed together as she reached to help. It felt so normal to feel the touch of his hand on hers. Then he reached up and softly ran his fingers down her cheek as he repositioned a curl of hair behind her ear.

"Thank you." She said.

"You're more than welcome."

The night was almost magical. There were other quickly shared moments. Always just a fleeting touch, a personal look, a wink of the eye or the smile that said, "I love what we're doing."

Was it true? Could Brad have feelings for her? How was that possible? And what if he did? Did she feel the same way? Noelle was instantly anxious.

"Father, is this a good thing or a bad thing? This could ruin everything that I have come to love. What if…"

"My daughter, do you trust me to take care of you?" She could feel the Father ask.

"Yes. But…"

"By faith, daughter. By faith."

"Yes Father."

Noelle was learning to live in that relation-ship mode with her Heavenly Father and it felt good. Trust Him. That was what she was going to do. Trust Him. Why? She would trust Him because…tomorrow morning when she woke up, He would be here with her. If she had a need…He would be here. If she needed a friend…He would be here. He would never leave her. She could tell Him all of her fears and joys. Noelle real-ized that she would never be alone again and the letters that this daddy had already written to her were full of love and direction. The letters that He had prepared for her would never leave her feeling lost and alone. She would never have to wonder about His love. He said, *"My daughter, I love you with an undying love and I made plans just for you and I know what those plans are. They will prosper you and not harm you. My plans will give you a hope and a future. Because I have earned your trust, you will call on Me, you will come to Me, and you will pray to Me. I will listen to you, you will want to seek me with all of your heart, and you will find me. I will never desert you or leave you lost and alone when the trials of life threaten to wash over you. I will be your mighty fortress and I will hide you in the shelter of my arms. I will be the covering that protects and shields you. I will hold your tears in my hands for I love you enough that I have counted the hairs on your head; that is how intimately I have loved you from the moment that I intricately knit you together in your mother's womb. I breathed life into you and these are just a few of the promises that I make to you. I will love you endlessly. I will be your God and you will be my daughter."*

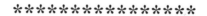

Brad's morning had an early start to it. He had some papers that he had to drop off at a farmer down the road who had purchased a young bull from him this week. He was leaving early to do that before his first morning class. Although, he would have much rather stayed and waited to see Noelle before he left.

He thought of last night. They were good thoughts; especially the soft feel of her hand in his. He thought that it was a perfect fit. The little bounce of her curls as they walked. The look in her eyes as he wrapped the scarf about her and kissed her head. Yes, the evening had gone well. Noelle seemed cautious as usual in the beginning; but he thought that he had seen her begin to let down her guard.

He was most excited about the conversation that they had about the baby. He wasn't sure what he would be feeling if she had answered differently. However, she did not. Noelle would like to keep her baby. Every day was a change in her. He could see her softening and putting away the anger and bitterness that she had worn so openly when she first came. He also could see her blossoming underneath the growing knowledge of Jesus Christ. God did have a plan and it was coming together nicely, if he did say so himself.

There were still those moments of almost panic when he would visualize himself with an instant family. Time was moving too quickly. Four more months and it would be July. There would be a baby born; out of wedlock. Brad was sure that was not what God's plan would be.

Being the planner that God created him to be, Brad was thinking about timing. This was the end of March. Next week would be the first week of April. He knew that Genie and Noelle's sisters would be coming for the week of spring break. He was excited to be meeting Noelle's sisters. He had not talked with Genie since the day that he took Noelle and her mom to the airport. So much had happened since then. Really, it had been such a short period; but life-changing preparation had been happening in the supernatural realm. God had been preparing Noelle for that moment when Brad would ask the question. He was sure of it. Anticipation was building inside of Brad. The protective spirit in him wanted to take care of her. That same feeling had welled up in him from that first moment when he saw her brokenness in the car. Now that he knew what God intended, he was ready to move forward. Still there were those moments of questions. *Was he ready to be a good husband? What did he know about being a father?* If he were going to be honest, he would admit that sometimes he wondered if he would have different feelings for this baby than he would for a child that was his own.

Those were the times that he would remind himself that there was no need to wonder. God was working it all out, so much better than Brad could. So relax and enjoy the journey.

A month of class and he was done for the year. Last year he took summer classes. Just yesterday, he decided that he would not be doing that this year. Summer was going to be full. He was becoming sure of that. There would be many changes. He did not want to miss any of them.

Birth was something that was familiar to him. The miracle of new life on the farm was something that happened often. Still, it never got old for Brad. He marveled at every new calf. They were all so different, perfectly mastered by the Father's hand.

This would be different. This new life was a gift that God had hand picked just for him, an innocent baby that he would need to nurture and love. In addition, Brad had dealt many times with the needs of a first time mommy. He did not mean to compare Noelle to the animals that he had nurtured for years; yet in so many ways, the compassion that was a part of his very soul had come from taking care of those animals. Brad had learned the importance of gentleness when it came to new life from those special moments that he witnessed and shared. He had earned the trust of the mommies long before their time had come to deliver with that same

PERFECT LOVE

gentle spirit.

Noelle would need to trust him. He would need to be gentle and love her.

He had originally seen Noelle as fragile and timid. Now he could see that there was a spunky side; a side that he thought…full of life. Brad also knew that Noelle would need to continue to heal. The wounds that her dad had left her with would need time. Trust had been broken. Despite the pain that was there, he saw a strength that reminded him of his mother.

He thought of his mother now with love. Brad had been old enough when his dad died to see the pain that had gripped his mom. It was a scary time for all of them. He remembered thinking, "What was their life going to look like?" It was the love of the Lord that carried them through and redefined their definition of family. He watched as his mother mourned. Then he watched as she put away her mourning for a more productive walk. Given the changes that were beyond her comprehension, she made a choice to move forward. She created a safe and happy home for them; yet honored the memory of the man that they all loved so much. Life had been good. Her life had taken on the strength of the Lord and she had shared that with her boys. Now he could see some of that in Noelle. It was baby steps and she was learning as she went. That was okay. Brad was a patient man. He knew that they would have a lifetime to work through all of it. He just was not sure when God would be ready. Of this he was sure…Brad was going to be ready when God said go.

That was the reason that today after class he was going to make a trip into downtown Indianapolis. There was a special jeweler that he had worked with over the years when there was a need. Today he had a need. It was a need that had to be filled just so. Perfect love. That's what it had to be.

Angelina was the only one in the kitchen when Noelle came down the stairs.

"Well good morning. I can see that the look on your face is the same as Brad's. Both of you were hoping to see someone who is not here. I wonder what that could all be about. Must be that some couple had a good night last night." Angelina teased Noelle as she slid into a stool across from her.

"Maybe. Just maybe." Noelle teased right back. "Brad must have left early this morning huh?"

"Yup. He had some errands to run before class. My guess is that you will see him when we all get home. He seems to be keeping pretty close to the house these days. Again, I can't help but wonder why that is?"

Noelle smiled an impish smile that made her look even more beautiful. "You seem to be full of questions today!"

Angelina laughingly patted Noelle's hand and said, "Oatmeal and toast today. Not just plain old oatmeal though. This has a little bit of everything in it. I sweetened it with pure maple syrup that comes from the trees on the farm. A nearby farmer collects the sap when it runs and then boils it down. He gives us some every year. This is the last of last season's syrup. Soon we will be getting a new batch; makes the hot cereal just a little better. There are also dried blueberries, from our own bushes here on the farm, cranberries, a little flax seed and I put a squirt of flax seed oil in to add that nutty flavor. Here is some whole-wheat toast and the spread is cream cheese with some of my homemade strawberry freezer jam stirred in. Do you want turkey bacon or turkey sausage?" Angelina asked her.

"Oh my goodness you do spoil me. I choose turkey sausage." Noelle answered.

"You got it." Angelina said as she opened a dish that had both options in it. She stabbed two pieces and placed them on Noelle's plate. "More?"

"No thank you...I don't know how I'm going to eat all of this." Noelle answered with a smile of gratitude.

Angelina began the speech that she had practiced in the mirror this morning thinking that she was being so sneaky. "So your mom has your ticket all set for you to fly home Wednesday. You can pick it up at the 'will call window' when you get to the airport. They are anxious to hear what happens at the doctor appointment. She called last night while you were out with Brad. I told her that the two of you had gone out to relax and that I had to practically push you out the door. I also told her that you work too hard. We talked for a while. She is very anxious to see you and so are the girls. They said that you are not very good about sending pictures of your belly. It's the talk of your home apparently."

Angelina sensed that Noelle was a little shy about the conversation that they were having.

She pressed on, "Honey, its okay to celebrate the stages of your pregnancy. God wouldn't want you to be embarrassed about the baby that you're carrying." Angelina pushed a little bit. This was her nature. Pushing did come easy for her. That was okay with Noelle. Angelina had earned the right. She had pushed her way into Noelle's life and had made sure that Noelle knew she did so because she cared.

"I know." Noelle shrugged. "It just seems funny broadcasting the fact that I'm pregnant. You know. Not being married and all. No one else knows the circumstances. I can only guess what people will think about me. Then I wonder about the stigma that'll be placed on the baby if I keep him…or her."

"Listen. This is not your fault. This is not the baby's fault. God does not make mistakes. He knew before the beginning of time about this little one and He sees the coming of His return, and things that seem too huge today; will seem like they do not matter tomorrow. Life is ever flowing and always changing. Do not spend energy dwelling on the past. Look toward the future. Four months and there will be a beautiful bundle of joy that will need you to be strong. No matter what direction life turns. Just listen for God. He always hears and He always answers. The answers are not always what we are looking for. That is why He is God."

Noelle nodded.

"Eat your breakfast. Let's try to leave here within 30 minutes. Will that work for you?" Angelina asked.

"I'm ready. I'll eat fast." Noelle said.

"Not too fast. My food is to be enjoyed and savored, not wolfed. Okay?"

"Besides…you don't want indigestion, that burning sensation is no fun."

Noelle laughed at Angelina's boldness. You never knew what she was going to say next.

Chapter Seven

Psalm 96:7

Ascribe to the LORD,

O families of nations,

Ascribe to the LORD

glory and strength.

DELMYN WOKE AND DID NOT HAVE A CLUE WHERE HE was, however, that in itself was not unusual for him these days. Lately, there had been too many parties with too much alcohol or other, shall we say, "Recreational substances". Last night had been the other. He tried not to indulge in the crazy stuff too often. It left him with too many questions. He kept trying to clear his vision. Everything was blurry. The noises were making his head hurt. He wished they would all shut up.

The ache in his back was beginning to throb. He had to move. What is this He wondered? I must be lying on a cement floor. That thought brought more clarity to him and he tried to move. As he did, he realized that he was lying on a slab and he did not have any clothes on, just his briefs.

"Where am I?" He must have spoken it aloud.

"Hey, sleeping beauty just woke up." He heard laughter; but they were voices that he did not recognize.

Trying again to open his eyes, he saw the matching outfits on men from across the room. They were all sitting together on another cement slab.

Panic began to roll through him as the unmistakable taste of the contents of his stomach surged up. It rose up and into his throat then came explosively out onto the floor as he rolled onto his side.

"OH NO! Gross! Man! Did you have to do that? There were other words echoed from the other men that were not pretty.

Trying to raise himself to a sitting position he whispered, "Where am I?" The acid burning his throat hindere d the sound coming from him. Trying to swallow, his throat so dry that it stuck together, he tried to say it again, this time louder and more impatiently as he tried to remember what he had done last night. "Where am I?"

"County jail Dude. It must have been one awesome party that got you here. You haven't been awake for two days. When they brought you in here, you weren't walking. We weren't sure the first day that you were even alive. The last twelve hours them demons been haunting you; we don't want any part of them so you just stay over there on your side."

Del could see that the person talking was big and not so good-looking. The look on his face told Del that he was not someone who should be crossed. In fact, he was downright scary. He knew this truth for sure; he wasn't in a good place. And he wanted a bath and some clothes.

"How do we get some service here?" He asked.

The other occupants in the small cell roared and acted as if he had just said the funniest thing.

They all started talking at once. "Call room service. See what they can do for you."

"What part of county jail did you not understand White Boy?" One of the others commented.

"Yah, this isn't Hotel 6. It's not have it your way. No one is gonna be serving you anything but a slice of ugly."

Del was beginning to get that he was in a mess. He had never been to jail before. Wasn't he supposed to get a phone call or something? He needed to get out of here and quick. He was sure that nothing good was going to happen to him in a place like this.

Afraid to open his mouth, he just sat in silence. Reality began to sink in as he replayed what they had

94

already said. Two days! Really? That would explain why the inside of his mouth felt like it had been glued together and his stomach was rumbling loud enough that the guys on the other side must have been able to hear it.

He didn't know how much time had gone by; but he was relieved to hear a uniformed police officer call his name, "Delmyn Whitehall? You awake yet?"

"Yes. Get me out of here. I want to make my phone call. I know my rights." Although it was going to be difficult trying to gain any respect standing in nothing but his briefs.

"Here. Put these on." The officer said as he threw them through the bars. "Be quick about it. You have a lawyer waiting on you."

Good. At least I'll get out of here. I need to get a shower. Instantly his next thought was about where the party would be tonight. However, he could not even remember where the one that landed him in the slammer had been.

The officer stood there looking at the disgusting mess on the floor. "Really? I'm sure you're friends here would have appreciated a little more control than that."

He told the others to stand back and called for the cell door to be open. Everyone did as they were told and they all kept their mouths shut. So did he.

From the walkway he heard, "Hey what about the mess he left on the floor?" And from someone else, "Yah! We need room service." Everyone laughed.

"I'll send the maid." Del answered back as he thought himself quite clever.

"Shut up!"

Apparently, the officer did not have much of a sense of humor.

He had quickly slipped into the bright orange, one-piece uniform that everyone seemed to be wearing. It made him laugh when he thought; at least you can tell who the bad guys are. He must have laughed aloud because the officer turned and gave him that look. You know the one that says they don't think that you're funny.

"You aren't going to be laughing pretty soon. You are about to find out that there isn't anything funny here."

They walked through another guarded area where another officer without showing any emotion frisked him and used a wand to scan his body. All of this seemed unreal. Maybe I am dreaming and I'll wake up soon.

The officer picked up the conversation from before, "If I were you, I would sober up fast. You are in some serious trouble young man. This is not going to be something that just goes away. You may have really done it this time." The officer finished as he opened a door and stood back so that Del could enter. The door slammed shut.

There, in front of him, stood a man in a fancy suit behind a table. He looked very professional. His white shirt was stiff; so stiff that Dell thought it might cut his neck.

"Mr. Whitehall, you can have a seat. We have some serious questions that need to be answered. I hope that you have some great ones. My name is Tempo Mohan. I will be representing you in this situation. I have been placed on retainer by your parents. Apparently one of your friends called them after you were arrested." He finished.

"I wish that they hadn't done that. Better if my parents didn't know. You know how all of that works, right?"

"No I can't say that I do. This was not my kind of life style. I did others things while I was in college. Like getting an education. That is why I am the attorney and you are in jail," Mohan stated very matter of fact.

"Whatever. What do we have to do to get me out of here? I've certainly been here long enough to sober up. Don't I just have to stay twelve hours? Those perverts in the cell told me that I've been here two days."

Tempo could feel his blood pressure rising. Taking a deep breath and counting to ten before he spoke, "You are under the misunderstanding that you are leaving here. That is not going to be happening today."

Becoming angry Del stated loudly, "What do you mean? I have to stay longer? I was not even driving. I don't think I was driving anyway." Again, Del tried to clear his mind enough to remember what had happened.

"Lower your voice." Tempo ordered in an authoritative way. This is not about sobering up. Can you tell me what you were doing at the time that all of this happened? What do you know about the girl that you were with?"

"Was I with a girl? I hope she was good looking. I would hate to go to jail over a dog!" Del finished softly chuckling to himself as if he thought himself quite clever.

"Mr. Whitehall. This is serious business. You are going to be charged with a felony. Rape. Do you understand what I'm saying?" Del's attention sharpened.

"Rape? Are you serious? Those girls are at all the parties. They come expecting some kind of action or they wouldn't be there. All I'm doing is accommodating them. You could say that I'm just performing a small service. And I do it for free."

"Girls? So you're telling me that there are going to be more coming forward?"

"Coming forward? What are you talking about?" Del was beginning to understand. His head was starting to clear. Even in his confused state, he was realizing that he was in big trouble.

"Mr. Whitehall, listen to me carefully. I need you to focus on what I am saying. A woman from a party has witnesses who have identified you as present, has alleged that you, with an accomplice, drugged her and then raped her." He paused giving Del time to process what he was saying and then continued. "This girl was taken to the hospital by the friend who is suggesting that she also was at the party and can testify that she took this girl from your bed and straight to the hospital."

The room was silent, again giving the young man time to understand what Tempo had said. He intently watched the expressions as they changed on the face across the table from him. It was a sobering thought and Del seemed to be getting the reality of the situation.

"How do they know it was me? There were lots of guys at the party." Del said.

"Understand this is all preliminary findings. I have not had time to compile all of the information yet. This is what is listed in the police reports. The second girl removed the girl pressing charges directly from your bed. They then went straight to the hospital. A hospital drug test confirmed that she had drugs in her system that according to her, she had not taken. The other girl, who also took a drug test and did not have drugs in her system, alleged that she had brought her own drink to the party. She signed a statement saying that neither of them had taken anything. An investigation began and the police were dispatched to the residence where they found you in bed under the influence of narcotics. You were removed and brought here. Where you will remain unless you can give me some information that disputes the evidence that the police have."

"How did you get involved?"

"Try to stay with me. Someone from the house called your parents, who after doing some checking, called me."

"So now my parents are in the middle of this. Well then, they will take care of it. Tell them to pay the fines and get me out. I'll just have to deal with them and everything will be fine."

Mr. Mohan was realizing the type of person with whom he was dealing. This was a family of wealth. Delmyn's father had made that clear when he talked with Teo. He said, "I am a man of prominence with friends in high places. I'm willing to pay whatever it takes to get my son out of here." More than once he heard, "Money is no object. Just get my son out. He doesn't belong there."

"I reassured your father that I would do everything that I could as quickly as possible. However, Mr. Whitehall..."

"Call me Del. My father goes by Mr. Whitehall. I'm just Del."

"Very well, Del," the name rolled off of Mr. Mohan's tongue almost as if it repulsed him, "getting you out of here isn't going to happen instantly. Tomorrow you will go before a judge and you will be arraigned. The official charges will be brought and you'll be given a chance to tell them how you plead."

"Why can't I go today?"

"Your arraignment has been court set for tomorrow. That's why you can't go today."

Del was starting to get frustrated. "What kind of an attorney are you if you can't make everything happen today? Geesh!"

Patiently Mr. Mohan looked very intently at Del and said, "I am a very good attorney. Moreover, it just so happens that you are going to need a good one. In addition, I am a good man. One who doesn't get himself into these types of situations, Del," Mohan said as he emphasized the name.

Del stared straight back at him and said, "Well tell them that I plead not guilty. Then sit back and watch my Dad at work. I will be out of here before you can blink. Are you that good?"

Teo wanted to reach across the table and shake the young man. He had young daughters who he wanted to protect from boys just like Delmyn Whitehall, boys who had no concern for anyone but themselves. Instead, he said, "I will see that you have clean clothes for the arraignment. I should have more information tomorrow. We will talk before you go in front of the judge. My suggestion to you for the rest of the time that you are sitting here is this…think about what you are doing and where you are in life. Is this who you want to be?"

With that said, Teo picked up his pad of paper, closing it into his briefcase and called for the officer to release him from the room.

Standing with his back to Del, he heard him say, "You just remember that my dad's money tells you what to say. You are replaceable."

Tempo Mohan looked back as the officer opened the door and saying nothing he smirked and walked out.

As they walked down the hall, the officer shook his head and said, "He's one of those guys."

Teo, as his friends called him, said with sadness, "I know; but God loves him."

✱✱✱✱✱✱✱✱✱✱✱✱✱✱✱

A different officer came for Del and took him to yet another cell. In this cell, he was by himself. There was a sink and a toilet; the slab was now gone and replaced by a bunk with a mattress. There was a sheet, blanket and pillow lying on top.

He took a few minutes to wash up and lay down on the bed, not even bothering to put the sheet on. He thought to himself, *not very comfortable. But, I guess that I've slept on worse.* He grimaced.

Alone in the cell, he had some time to think. He supposed that this time he had gotten himself in real trouble. His biggest concern was that he was going to have to deal with his dad. That wasn't going to be very much fun. His mom would help with that though. She always did. She loved him the most. He could always count on her to be on his side. His dad would scream, throw fits and be angry for a while. Then mom would bring him around. Life would slowly return to normal. That's the pattern. Del would just have to lay low and give his dad time to cool down. It might take longer this time. Bigger money was probably involved now. Dad had paid for Del's mistakes before. It just never involved the police and it was never huge money. He assumed that this was going to be a good chunk of money.

Too bad, he thought aloud, *I just wasted a pile of my inheritance. Good thing there's more where that came from.*

Del wondered about the girl. Straining, some of his memory was returning. He was trying to picture what she looked like. He could remember that his brain was already fuzzy when they brought her into the bedroom. Try as hard as he could, there just was not any memory past the point of her coming into the room. Was there only one girl that night? He could not even remember that. He was trying to remember what pills he had popped. They must have been some good stuff to erase everything even after two days here without waking up. That cannot be good. He thought, *maybe he had better slow down on all of that for the time being. Give his life a rest before something crazy happens.*

He chuckled to himself as he realized that he was in jail. *"Something crazy has already happened."* He said aloud.

He tried to remember everything that the attorney had said. He said, "Me, with an accomplice." *Does that mean that someone else was busted too? Well there better be someone else. I am not going to take the blame for this all by myself. Who was dishing out the candy? All I did was my male duty to service. Since when had that become a crime? It wasn't as if they had to pay me. No one was holding them down and stealing their money. I wasn't taking anything that they didn't give away all the time. Right?"*

His thoughts ventured into the future. *What if this ridiculous charge goes to trial? That could be pretty embarrassing having my mom hear some of this stuff. She'll be pretty sad. I'll just have to tell her that it's not true. I may have to do some kissing up. She'll be okay. She loves me enough for that. I'm her little boy. She won't let anything bad happen to me. She'll fight for me. She'll probably have to fight dad on this one. But, she will. After all, I am the favored son. I'm all that she has. I'm pretty sure that she'll choose me over dad."*

On that note, with nothing better to do, Del grabbed the blanket and threw it over him. He dozed off to sleep as if he did not have a care in the world.

Chapter Eight

Psalm 96:8

Ascribe to the LORD the glory due

His name;

Bring an offering and come into His courts

FRIDAY NIGHT WAS A BUSTLE OF ACTIVITY AT THE Smith home. They were all doing laundry and filling suitcases and bags as it came out of the dryer. The excitement was building. Genie and the girls could not wait to be on the road and headed to surprise Noelle. It felt like it had been forever. This was the first separation for any period of time and three months felt like an eternity.

The girls had so much to share with her. She had missed everything in their school year. Volleyball season was just finishing up and softball season was gearing up.

Nothing had seemed right this year, or last year for that matter. There was an uneasiness that filled their every day. When their dad left, it had created too many changes. Nothing felt like a safe place. Although they had to admit that since they had been praying for their dad every day, that part of their life had gotten easier. The truth was in praying for him their anger and bitterness was receding and they were finding a healthier place to live. Not that they were understanding what happened any better; but they realized that God was going to take care of all of that mess. By putting it in God's hands, they did not have to dwell on it all of the time. They were learning to trust God, even if they didn't realize that was what was happening.

On the days that Genie was being completely honest with herself, the girls were coming to that place of peace with their dad better than she was. She did not let them know that. Nights were still so long for her. Even praying, she was still not at a spot where she could just leave the questions for God. Why did he leave her with so many open doors that she couldn't seem to close. In Genie's mind, it just seemed like there was so little closure. How was she ever going to find the answers that she searched her mind for every night? She was trying to build her faith to a point of trusting. The good news was just that...THE GOOD NEWS! Now she knew that she could talk to the Heavenly Father and He would never leave her.

They were still looking for the perfect church for their family. It was harder than they thought. They wanted some area of their life to fit again, some place that felt like they belonged. Maybe they were being too critical. After what they had been through, they probably were guarded. After all, who would want to open themselves up and allow anyone in that could hurt them again. Their life was a basket full of wounds and they were trying to work through all of that. It just was going to take some time, one wound at a time.

Tonight there was giddiness in the house. They felt like little girls before Christmas morning. Only this present was a trip to be with Noelle. They were going to have one whole week to talk and laugh. They planned to do lots of shopping. They had been looking at baby clothes. Everything was so sweet. However, the girls had been disappointed when their mom would not let them buy anything yet. Genie was waiting to see what Noelle was thinking about the baby. Was she bonding or was she thinking about adoption?

They all accepted that this decision was Noelle's to make. However, the thought of the baby was like playing house when they were little. They all wanted to be the mommy and not the sister or aunt. It was more fun being the mommy. Only this time Noelle's heart would be forever wrapped up in this new role and no matter what decision she made, there would always be heart ties. Genie had told the girls more than once through their conversations, once a mommy…always a mommy, no matter what.

Genie had realized the excitement that was brewing over the baby. It concerned her some. She did not want the girls to glamorize the pregnancy or the baby. Being the sole provider for a newborn or any age child would always be a struggle. There was not anything easy about what Noelle was facing. She wanted the girls to understand all of that. Babies are cute and sweet; but remembering back, they have their ugly side too. Then there is the expense. How will Noelle carry all of that by herself?

When Genie began to think along those lines, she would quickly reel back in her thoughts. She would take a breath and remind herself that God is in control. He is working through everything in His time. He has a plan, a plan to prosper them. They have to stand on His word and keep their eyes on him and not on the circumstances.

"Mom! Where are you?" Nissa was yelling.

"In here," she called back as she loaded the last load into the dryer.

"Mom, Anaya and I don't want to wait until tomorrow. Can't we leave tonight? Please?" There was a whining tone to her voice.

Anaya chose that moment to make her own appearance and with the same whining, she enumerated the same message. "Please Mom? We could be there in the morning. It would be one more day with Noelle. The time is already going to go so fast."

Genie started to say no and stopped. She wanted to see her daughter as bad as the girls did. So thinking

107

for a moment she offered, "How about if we get started and drive until I get tired. Then we could stop for the night, get a hotel and start again in the morning. That would get us in earlier. Does that sound better?"

"Yah! Awesome!" The girls were jumping up and down and dancing around Genie. She was laughing at them. The laundry room was not that big so it was a small dance floor.

"Listen", Genie said. "It'll be 40 minutes before this load comes out of the dryer. I think we all have clothes in here that we want to take. If you get every-thing around and these are the last items to go in the bags, we could be on the road in an hour maybe. We can grab something to eat on the road. What do you girls think?"

"We're all packed and we'll just throw the dryer stuff on top. So why don't we just go make sandwiches and we'll eat here. Then we don't have to waste the time to eat on the road. Okay?"

"Sounds good to me. Just make sure that you clean everything back up in the kitchen. I've already got that room ready for us to be gone." Genie cautioned.

"We will." They chimed.

"Plus we'll pack up some snacks for the car. If we eat, we'll be able to stay awake longer." Anaya said.

Genie knew where this was going, "Hey…just so we are clear, I'm not driving all night. I would waste my first day with Noelle if I lose a whole night of sleep. Got it?"

"Yes Mom." They answered; but Genie could see that they were conspiring. They thought that they could change her mind. Who knew, maybe they could.

One hour on the dot, they were locking up the door and getting in the car. Genie was sure that they could not have possibly put that load of clothes away that quickly. She did not look; but she was sure if she did, she would find them tossed on their bed or some other place. The girls had not only supposedly put away their clothes; but came to her room and helped put her clothes away also. When Genie left her room, everything was neat and tidy; no clothes on the bed.

While that last load was drying, the girls had made sandwiches that they all ate quickly. They had cut up veggies to have with them. It almost felt like a picnic as they crunched on apples for dessert. The excitement was energetic as they both talked at once.

Driving down the road for a while Genie asked, "What do we have to drink?"

Trying to conceal their giggling, Anaya pulled a cold, bottle of pop out of the bag and handed it to her.

"Oh no you don't! If I drink caffeine this late, I will never get to sleep. I can see completely through your plan and it isn't going to work. What else do you have?" Genie asked handing the pop back.

"Water!" Nissa said sadly.

"That will do for now. Thank you." Genie said as she took the water.

A couple hours on the road and the girls were settling in. They were making good time, especially when you take into consideration that they had left at 6:30 and caught the tail end of rush hour traffic. There had not been any slow downs and Genie had set the cruise at 72. She was willing to push the speed limit a couple of miles. However, that was it. She did not need a ticket.

An hour later, as they were cruising down the road, Nissa suggested to Genie, "You know Mom; I could help you drive if you are feeling like you need a break. I could drive for a while and you could grab a little sleep. Then maybe you could drive and I could sleep. We could team drive."

Genie looked at her middle daughter and smiling at her sweetly said, "Nissa, do you actually think that I could turn this car over to you with the experience that you have, late at night, close my eyes and go to sleep?"

Nissa prepared to build a case when Anaya jumped in, "Forget it Nissa. We are going to stop for the night."

The girls went quiet as Genie offered, "Sorry girls. I do know how excited you both are, but safety first."

At 10:30, the excitement of the day was starting to wear on Genie. She noticed that the girls were starting to doze off. Just down the road was a hotel and she pulled off. The girls were tired enough that they did not give her any complaint. Quickly they checked into their room. Brushing their teeth, they got into bed and asked if they could have a 6:00 a.m. wake up call. Genie agreed. Anaya made the call to the service desk and shortly after that, the girls were sound asleep in the other bed.

It was not that easy for Genie. Sleep eluded her as usual. Her mind continued to think about Noelle. Time was moving so quickly. Four months would be gone before they knew it. Noelle was going to have to make decisions. Was she planning to stay in Indianapolis after giving birth or would she come home? If she came home, would it be with a baby or without? Genie's mind began to jumble with too many questions and thoughts.

Enough! She ordered. Genie decided it was time for her to pray, *"Our Father in heaven, hallowed be Your name, Your kingdom come, Your will be done on earth as it is in heaven. Give us today our daily bread. Forgive us our debts, as we also have forgiven our debtors. And lead us not into temptation, but deliver us from the evil one. For Thine is the kingdom, and the power, and the glory forever. Amen."*

The Lord's Prayer had become such a comfort to Genie. It covered all principles of life. There was a calming in her spirit when she repeated it. Sometimes, she would voice it line by line and in between would stop as she made it more personal to her daily requests.

Our Father in heaven, hallowed be Your name;

I worship you Father. You deserve all praise and honor.

Your kingdom come, Your will be done on earth as it is in heaven.

I ask that today You give me kingdom mentality. Help me to know what Your will for my life is and to walk towards You as I go through this day.

Give us today our daily bread.

Everything that I have comes from you. You supply all of my needs and I thank you for your blessings.

Forgive us our debts, as we also have forgiven our debtors.

I am sorry for any sins that I have committed. Please forgive me. I forgive anyone who I feel has wronged me, hurt me, or come against me. I give those feelings to You to take to the cross on my behalf.

Lead us not into temptation; but deliver us from evil.

Father, keep me from sin. And keep the evil one and his snares far from me and those that I love. Help me to walk in Your ways always.

For Thine is the kingdom, and the power and the glory forever. Amen.

This world belongs to You. I belong to You. You

hold the keys that unlock all power here. I am Your daughter and You have set me in higher places. I will worship You forever. Amen.

Genie would find herself repeating that throughout the day. It would give her a peace and refocus her on her Savior. Life has a tendency to get in the way and when it does, we start to take our eyes off the Maker of all things. It only takes a moment to repeat the prayer. However, the peace that it brings is that **'peace that surpasses all understanding'**. The prayer is Genie's lifeline in the storms.

Genie closed her eyes and after repeating the prayer through a couple of times, that peace began to flood through her and she felt her eyes become heavy as she slowly drifted off to sleep.

✶✶✶✶✶✶✶✶✶✶✶✶✶✶✶✶

"What is that strange ringing?" Genie could feel the sound pulling her from somewhere far off. Opening her eyes, she realized where she was. Grabbing the phone she answered, "Hello."

"This is your wake up call. Have a great day." The voice on the other end of the phone said.

"Thank you and you also." Genie hung up as she realized that she was talking to an automatic voice system.

Suddenly she realized, *I slept through the whole night. Wow. When was the last time that happened?* She wondered to herself.

Looking into the other bed, reality set in that the girls were gone. Alarm began to run through her body. Adrenalin surged through her system. They were in a strange place. She didn't know …

Just then, she heard the door key and the girls entered the room, carrying plates of food from the continental breakfast bar downstairs in the lobby.

"Good morning." They said.

"Good morning. You gave me quite a scare when I woke up and you were gone." Genie said.

"Sorry Mom. You were sleeping so soundly. You didn't even hear us getting around. We've taken showers and done our hair and we're ready to leave." Nissa said.

"You mean you did all of that while I slept and I didn't even wake up. That's amazing." Genie puzzled.

"We know. You don't sleep very well anymore." Nissa said.

"We hear you sometimes." Anaya added as she shrugged her shoulders at the questioning look from her mother.

Their words caught her off guard, "I'm sorry. I thought I was careful not to worry you girls with that."

Anaya sat down beside her and putting her arm around her mom's shoulders said with lightness, "How many times do we have to remind you that we are a team? Huh?"

Genie lovingly tickled her youngest daughter as she squirmed to escape.

"Uh…hey! Have you both forgotten that we have somewhere to be as soon as we can get there?" Nissa said holding up the plate of food that she was carrying.

Catching Genie off guard, Anaya gave one last tickle and jumped off the bed. "Eat up!" She ordered.

Genie obeyed.

Everything done and they were on the road before 7:00 a.m. The girls tried to talk Genie into taking a shower when they got to Angelina's but Genie laughed at them as she turned on the water. "I'll be fast!" She said. Noelle had Genie's hair. She could just run some gel through it and the curls would just fall into place and bounce through the day that way. She wore very little make up. She was a beautiful woman. Careful only to use natural oils on her face with just a little mascara and she was ready for the day. She had always stressed to the girls that they needed to take care of their skin. She would say, "Natural beauty comes from taking care of the inside of you. Remember, this is the only skin that you will have. You want it to last a lifetime."

The girls were amazed at how great their mom looked compared to some of their friends' moms. Then, Genie never smoked or drank and she always made them drink lots of water. Only occasionally were they allowed pop or sugary drinks. "Not good for you. You will appreciate it someday." She would say. They could only hope to look as good as she looked when they reached her age.

The girls switched seats after they had filled the car up and they began to calculate their arrival time.

"Five hours. That should get us there by noon." Nissa said sitting in the front watching the map on the GPS.

"Well hold on. We will have potty breaks in there. Plus, we don't know where Noelle will be. I will have to call Angelina in a little bit and let her know that we are coming in early. They may be at the restaurant and that puts us another 20 minutes farther away." Genie cautioned the girls not to get excited about a noon arrival time.

"Call now." Anaya said. I think Angelina will be up. Anyway, you want to catch her before Noelle is up and hears her. Right?"

Genie thought about that for a minute. "Maybe

114

you're right. Angelina is an early riser. Will you please give me my phone?"

Nissa was quick to obey. She found the number and pushed the call button before her mom could change her mind. As she handed the phone to Genie, it was just a moment before they heard her say, "Good Morning."

Angelina must have asked if they were on the road yet; because Genie laughed and said that the girls had been so anxious that they had left last night and had driven part way. She said that they were about 5 hours out.

"Do you think that we should come to the restaurant?" Genie asked.

"That's fine." The girls' heard Angelina's answer through the phone.

"I'm guessing that we'll be there sometime around 1:00. That's going to put us there right in the middle of your lunch crowd. I'll try to slow these girls down some. But I haven't had much luck so far."

Genie laughed about something that Angelina had said. "We'll see you when we get there. As you can tell, we are very excited. Have a great day and say hi to the boys for us. It seems like so long since I have seen you and Noelle. We can't wait to hold our girl."

Another laugh and she said, "Bye for now." and hung up the phone. Handing the phone back to Nissa she said, "Okay, the restaurant it is."

"I was hoping that Angelina would just tell her not to go to work today." Anaya said. "Then we could have seen her right away."

"Noelle is a working girl now. There are people who depend on her. Besides, what reason would she have given her for not letting her go to work today? We're the ones that wanted to surprise her." Genie chided. "The time will go fast. We'll just make it. If we stop a little more often and get there, say between 2:00-3:00, lunch hour will be winding down and maybe we could get some time with her.

The girls didn't grab onto that idea so Genie just backed off the speed that she was driving and took a more leisurely pace. It would not make a huge difference; but it would help some.

She stretched the time as long as she could. A traffic jam from a small accident added 20 minutes to their arrival time. At 1:50 p.m., they walked into the restaurant and asked the hostess to seat them in Noelle's area if possible. They explained that they were her family and that they wanted to surprise her.

It worked perfectly. Noelle was out of the room when they entered. She was filling a salad order. The hostess, who introduced herself as Michelle, reminded Genie that they had met once before, seated them and they quickly hid behind menus she offered.

When Noelle walked up to the table she said, "Hi, my name is Noelle and I'll be your server today. Could I start you off with something to drink?"

Everyone pulled down their menus from their faces and said, "Just you!"

The look on her face was precious; total shock. As the girls jumped out of their seats, the tears were flowing down Noelle's face and instantly they were all hugging. The people in her room were watching what was playing out and they all began to clap and cheer.

Noelle quieted the crowd with her hands and announced, "This is my mom and sisters from out of town." To the girls she said, opening her arms wide to include the whole room, "This is everyone."

Laughs surrounded them as people said, "Hi

116

Mom, Hi Girls." and quieted back to the business of eating their lunch.

"What are you doing here?" Noelle questioned them.

"We're surprising you." Nissa said.

"We're going to spend the whole break with you. It was Angelina's idea. We're going to be staying at the farm." Anaya said.

Noelle looked at her mom. "It's true. Angelina insisted and so we're here."

Noelle was so excited. She did not know what to say.

Just then, Angelina, hearing all of the laughing and commotion, came forward to welcome them and officially meet the girls.

After introductions and hugs were out of the way, Angelina said to Noelle, "Why don't you stop and eat with your family. I'll cover the rest of your shift."

"No. I will finish the rest of my shift. Besides, I've heard that this table will be big tippers and I need their money." Noelle laughed.

"Come on. I am more than willing to do that for you. Your mom is going to think that I'm a slave driver." Angelina pleaded.

"Absolutely not! We have all week. I'll finish my shift." Noelle insisted this time.

"She is as stubborn as a mule and works too many hours. Maybe you can talk some sense into her." Angelina gave Noelle a quick hug as she went back to the kitchen.

"Now, what would you all like to drink?" Noelle asked the family that she loved so much.

Chapter Nine

Psalm 96:9

Worship the LORD

in the splendor of His

holiness;

Tremble before Him,

all the earth

BRAD WAS ON HIS WAY HOME AND HE WAS ABOUT to burst. He could just shout. In fact he did. He let out a whoop that the car in front of him probably heard. He had never been so sure about anything before. This was right. God had led him from the very beginning and he knew that God was still in control. He was just being obedient. Brad had found peace in every step that he had taken. He was just walking through the steps. Next step, he was going to find some time alone with his mom. He wanted her to know what he was about to do and why. He did not anticipate any objections from her. She knew him well enough to know that he would not be making a move this serious unless he was sure that God was leading him.

The timing was perfect. Noelle's family was in town and he would have the opportunity to talk with her mom before he asked Noelle the question. He didn't know Genie well enough to know if she would see this as a positive solution or an impulsive, spontaneous move. After all this did have the appearance of a fast decision. He understood Genie's situation with the circumstances at hand. Brad was sure that her first choice would not have been to have her daughter across states from her at a time like this. All of this and more had happened so quickly that she had to accept many changes in a life that seemed to have been evolving into something that she had not expected her life to resemble. Brad was going to have to trust God. He was sure that God had been preparing Genie, at the same time that He had been preparing Noelle and himself. He certainly was not going to start worrying about it now.

He said, *"God, I've tried to be obedient in every move of this journey. You have paved the way from beginning to end. I am asking that You continue doing that with Noelle's mom. Help her to understand Your plan. Help her to see that I am ready to love her daughter and the baby that she is carrying. It is only through You that any life changes like these can succeed. I know that yesterday, today and tomorrow You are always the same and that time has no relevance with You. Father, I rest in Your protective hand. Your will be done. Amen."*

And, that was that for Brad. Laying it in the Father's hands took all of the worry out of it. God was in charge and Brad knew that everything would be fine doing it God's way.

The ringing of a phone pulled him back from his wanderings. Looking, he saw that it was his mom. "Hey Beautiful!" He answered.

Angelina laughed and said, "Stop it!"

"Okay"

"No don't stop it. I miss hearing that from your father. It's nice. You can keep it up." She said.

There wasn't any sadness in her voice; but it did cause Brad to think about the times that his mom must miss the man that she had loved so much.

He lightened the conversation with, "What's up?"

"I just wanted to let you know that Noelle's family has arrived. They so completely pulled it off that Noelle was totally surprised. However, she is insisting on finishing her shift and so she's told the girls to head back to the house to settle. They should be at the house very soon. I'm hoping that you are close enough to welcome them properly and help to make them feel comfortable. I am going to try to get Noelle out of here early. That girl sure doesn't make it easy to help her with anything. She's such an independent little thing. Some man is going to have his hands full." Angelina finished with her usual "I love you" and was gone.

His mom's phone call brought a smile to his lips. His mom was right about that. It was going to be a lot of fun and frustration working to build a life with Noelle. The stubborn streak in her made her a survivor and a true helpmate, for him. We are all promised trials and tribulations from time to time. The enemy is real and comes attacking. You want to know that the person who stands by your side is strong enough to be there through thick and thin. Noelle has that strength. Brad had seen that determination in her from the first day in that stranded car on a dark, rainy road. When you add a little 'sassy' to the mix, it just makes it more fun.

Yup. Brad was excited with the turn that his life had just taken. He was ready to ride this one out to wherever God decided to take them.

He was almost at the farm now. If he didn't beat them there, then he should certainly be right behind them. They could settle in and be ready to catch up with Noelle by the time she returned home. He was secretly glad for the time alone with them. This would be his first conversation with Noelle's sisters. He saw this as opportunity to find out more about who she was and what made her tick.

Brad had gone into the barn to check on a few things and keep an eye out for the girls. He had only been there a few minutes when he saw their car pull into the drive. By the time that the car had stopped, Brad was opening Genie's door and offering his hand. He helped her out of the car and gave her a warm hug.

"It's so nice to have you back. Noelle has really

121

missed you."

Genie patted Brad's back, "Thank you. It's good to be back. I have missed her so much more than I could even begin to tell you. Let me introduce her sisters to you."

Before the girls got out of the car, they gave each other the look.

Anaya said, "Oh my gosh! Brad Conroy is one good-looking Indiana boy. Noelle could not have picked a better spot to have car trouble. Lucky her!"

Nissa shushed her and then whispered, "Maybe the guys back home need to eat more corn!"

They giggled as they got out of the car and came around to Genie's side of the car and Brad stretched out his arm and shook the offered hands.

Genie put her arm around her second daughter's shoulders, "This is Nissa. She's my middle daughter." Wrapping her other arm around her youngest she said, "This is Anaya. She's our baby."

Anaya rolled her eyes and with a smile on her face said, "Oh Mom!" To Brad she said, "I'm afraid that I'll always be the baby. But it's nice to finally meet you."

"We can't tell you how much we appreciate all that your family has done for our family. Not only have you offered Noelle a safe home; you've offered us all the opportunity to rejoice in an eternal home. We didn't know how much God loved us." Nissa said.

Brad, overcome with emotion, didn't know what to say. He was face to face with a family of mature women. They were women who loved God. He would want his children to have this heritage, a family that would nurture small children into adulthood with the reverence for the Lord.

Thank You God and praise Your holy name. Your

mercy never ceases to amaze me. "It has all just been the favor of God on all of our lives." Was all that Brad could say. The girls did not know that he really was praying a prayer of thanksgiving for them and the life that they were going to build together.

Pulling himself together his laugh lightened the moment, "Come on. Let's get you set up before Noelle returns so that you can really enjoy your time with her. Mom is going to try to pry her out of the restaurant early. She is one stubborn cookie. She would work more than Mom if that's possible." Brad grabbed some of the bags and helped them all into the house.

The girls were in awe at what they saw as they entered. What a place. They could certainly understand now what Genie had tried to tell them. No wonder Noelle was doing so well here. The peace flooded through you as soon as you entered the door. They were excited to share a part of this family.

Brad ushered them up the stairs. "You are welcome to do this anyway that makes you the most comfortable." Stopping in the middle of the hallway Brad said, "This is Noelle's room. Mom's room is at that end of the hall and there are these three rooms. You're welcome to set up any where that you want." Brad set the luggage down in the hall and opened the other three bedroom doors. "These three rooms don't have their own bathroom. You'll have to share this bathroom." He said as he opened the door between two of the rooms.

"How about I just leave you to make up your minds and I'll head back out to the barn to get everything done early. I am anxious to spend some time getting to know you better. Sound okay?"

"Okay!" The girls chimed in together. They were more than happy to spend time getting to know this hunk of a guy.

Brad laughed as Genie shook her head with a grin. "The girls seem to be happy with their options. Thank you again Brad for everything. As always, you're too kind."

"If I may intrude on some of your time Genie, maybe you and I could have some time to talk privately before Noelle gets here, if that would be all right with you?" Brad asked.

"Absolutely…I would love that." Genie said. In the back of her mind, a red flag went up. She couldn't help but wonder if everything was okay with Noelle.

Brad immediately sensed her unease. "Don't go borrowing trouble. Everything is fine. Noelle is doing great. Nothing to start worrying your pretty momma head about."

The girls laughed at his cute little accent, as he instantly made light of the situation. Still, they too couldn't help but wonder what was up with a "private" conversation.

"Make yourself at home and enjoy every minute of your stay with us. We wouldn't want it any other way." Brad said as he tipped his hat and headed down the stairs.

The girls were looking at each other giggling as they heard Brad step down the stairs and close the door softly behind him.

"Pretty momma head? That is the cutest little twang that I've ever heard." Anaya was almost swooning.

Nissa added, almost breathless, "I think I'm in love." Turning to her mother she added, "Can I marry him? Please? Please?"

Genie laughed at her girls. "You girls try to pull

yourselves together and let's get settled and ready for Noelle to get home."

Nissa walked into the first room. It was quaint. Soft blues were everywhere. The bed was a simple full size bed with a beautiful bed quilt on it. All different blue tones pulled together making a beautiful print picture. "I'll take this room." She said.

Anaya asked, "How can you decide without seeing the other rooms?"

"If it doesn't get any better than this, I can't go wrong." She answered.

"Oh you girls! Genie softly scolded. You just decide where you are going and put my bags into the left over room. I am going into the bathroom and then down to the barn to find Brad. We'll have that talk before Noelle gets here that way for sure.

"Okay Mom. Make sure you remember everything that he says. We're going to want a detailed recount."

Genie looked at her youngest daughter and said, "He said private and I think the invitation was delivered to me." She smiled as she closed the bathroom door leaving the two girls staring at the spot where she used to be.

"What do you think that's all about?" Nissa looked to her sister.

"I don't know. Kind of mysterious huh?" Anaya puzzled as she opened the door to the next bedroom. This room was all in greens, very springy. The walls were a sage with soft, white filmy curtains that had the same color of sage leaves embroidered on them. Scattered

125

through out the room on walls were pictures of billowing grasses dancing in the wind. The yellows of sunlight streaked throughout the pictures.

"Nissa look." Anaya said. "The room is just as beautiful as the first one.

Together they opened the third door. This room was at the end of the hall and was darker and richer colored than the first two. The walls were burgundy with grey trim on all the windows and doors. Beautiful and elegant.

The girls looked at each other and said at the same time, "Mom's." They pulled her case into the room and went back to their own rooms to do just what Brad had said…make themselves at home.

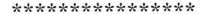

Genie freshened herself and headed to the barn. The crisp country air was invigorating on her face. The sun was so nicely peaking through the leaves that were just starting to erupt on the trees and she could hear the sound of birds singing as she walked. The squirrels ignored her as they continued their games of chase. She marveled to herself, what a beautiful place Lord you have created. Thank you again for dropping my family into this Garden of Eden.

Genie found Brad shoveling out the stall of a mommy cow and her calf. He didn't hear her approach. However, she could hear him.

"There you go momma. Take care of your baby. She needs you. She came a little early. You and I are gonna make sure that she gets a good start. I'll gather some good food with some extra vitamins. You'll both be fine." Brad said to the animals that both looked up at

126

him with large, adoring eyes. Genie wasn't even sure if cows could 'adore'. These two sure appeared to have that look that said the sun rose and set on the man in front of them.

As he was patting the animals he heard, "You really love what you do don't you?" Genie startled Brad.

Taken by surprise, he seemed a little embarrassed. "I sure do." was all that he said though. "I knew from the first time that I could come out here with my dad that I wanted to be here. Now my brother, he doesn't want anything to do with the farm. He's destined to find some mission field where he can plant a different kind of seed. He has a passion for the Lord and lost people. He's also a man looking for adventure. I find all of the adventure that I want right here. Look at these two. Who could not love them?" Brad lovingly stroked both mommy and baby.

"Is there a problem with them?" Genie asked.

"There isn't anything serious, just a little one. Momma was having some trouble towards the end. I'm not sure why. The calf came a little early. I locked them up in here to give them some extra time. Momma can nurture her baby and I can monitor everything a little bit closer. They will be fine. God and I are watching out for them." The calf nuzzled his leg and Brad again patted his side.

Genie laughed as the calf jumped and whirled around at the playful pat.

"See what I mean…almost good as gold."

Brad took Genie's arm and carefully led her to a couple of chairs that sat in the entrance to the barn. He offered her a chair and positioned his chair so that he was sitting opposite her.

"Can I tell you a little something about who I

am?" He asked.

"I would like that very much." Genie answered.

"I grew up here from day one. Mom and Dad brought my brother and me up to see the importance of family. Our home was full of love. We were crushed when we lost my dad unexpectedly. But Dad had given enough of himself that we knew who we were and that we would be okay."

Brad paused for a moment as if to reflect on his dad. Genie could see the love that he had for him. She could also see how much he missed him.

Brad looked up, "He taught us the most important stuff. He taught us about God and His love for us. And he taught us to wait on God."

Brad was looking deep into Genie's eyes. As if saying that he needed her to understand what he was about to say. "Mrs. Smith, I've waited on God. I have not been a guy prone to dating just to date. I haven't had any serious relationships. Do not get me wrong. I like girls." Then he smiled at her as he lightened the mood.

"I've just always known that God had that one special girl waiting for me. I knew that He had created one that was going to walk through this life with me and be by my side through the good times and the bad. I knew that girl was worth the wait. I've asked God to help me be patient while I waited. He has and I have been."

Genie was beginning to wonder where Brad was going with all of this.

Brad looked down at his hand for a moment as if to pull his thoughts together. Then he continued, "I knew from that first moment when I saw Noelle, as desperate as she looked, that she was different. One look at her and an immediate need to protect her sprung up inside of me. I didn't understand that emotion at the time. I had only felt it before with my mom. I knew she was in my life for a reason. Why, I didn't know until recently."

"I talk to God and I try to follow His lead. He has never led me down a wrong path. I know now that God has brought Noelle to me to be that life mate."

Genie took a quick breath. She looked at Brad. "Are you saying that…?"

"I'm saying that I love your daughter and I think that I have from that first moment. I am saying that I have been very cautious with her; because she has decisions that only she can make and I don't want to influence them. However, I have talked enough with her to know that she wants to be this baby's mother. What is holding her back is that she isn't sure it's best for the baby to be raised by a single mom. She has no idea how I feel about her."

Brad paused giving Genie time to gather in all that he had shared, "I am saying, that with your permission, I'm going to ask Noelle to marry me…as soon as possible for both her and the baby. And for me."

Genie was speechless. She could honestly say that she did not see this one coming.

"Does Noelle have…feelings for you?" Genie didn't even know if love was the right word.

"I don't know. But I have to believe God has been preparing her just as He's been preparing me."

Genie ventured on cautiously, "What about the baby? This baby came from another man. Can you honestly say that you could love this child as your own?" Looking at Brad, Genie already knew the answer.

"Yes." He smiled as he nodded his head. "I'm already thinking that I might be partial to a little girl that looks just like her momma."

Genie began to cry as she shook her head. "I've wondered if anyone would ever love my daughter with the love that I see in you." A tear slowly slipped down her cheek. "She's a good girl."

Brad reached over and squeezed her hand. "Yes. Yes she is. She is one of a kind. God made her just for me. We're a fit. Then why wouldn't we be, He made her from my side. He created her with my rib. I'm already thanking God for the abundant life that He's creating for us as a family."

Genie paused, "What if she says no?"

Brad laughed shaking his head, "She won't. God would not have brought me this far if He wasn't working her towards the same goal. He would have put us on different roads. When our efforts are the foundation, we may fail. When His efforts are the foundation, we cannot fail. Our God has a plan. We just have to seek him."

Genie could not do anything but let the tears roll down her cheeks as she looked at the amazing young man across from her.

Brad gave her a moment as he went to find a box of tissues to offer her. As she wiped her tears away she asked, "You said soon."

"Yup, I did."

"What do you mean by soon?" Genie asked.

"Well I'm thinking that we'll all go on a picnic to the park on Sunday and with your permission, I'm going to find a way to ask her there. I am going to suggest that we have a wedding before you all go back home next week."

"Next week? Is that even possible?"

Brad smiled his big smile and said, "With God all things are possible."

Genie thought for a moment and then leaned over

and kissed his cheek softly. Squeezing his hands firmly, with tears in her eyes she answered, "If Noelle says yes, you have my permission to love my daughter forever."

"Forever." Brad said as he wrapped her into his arms of compassion.

Chapter Ten

Psalm 96:10

Say among the nations,

"The LORD reigns."

The world is firmly

established, it cannot be moved;

He will judge the peoples with

equity

NOELLE COULD HARDLY WAIT AS THEY DROVE home. The distance between the restaurant and home had never seemed so long. She was so excited to see her mom and

sisters. What a surprise. She had no idea. Could it have been only 3 months since she had seen them? Really? It seemed like so much more. She loved their surprise.

When they pulled into the drive, Angelina said, "Why don't you hurry in and I'll find Brad to help with the bags of food." She had packed up lots of extras so that they had plenty of food for the week ahead. She really wanted to be able to spend time with Noelle's family and get to know them.

"No. I can help you." Noelle said.

"Absolutely not! I'm putting my foot down on this one. You go. No more stalling. Why, land sakes, a person would think that you aren't anxious to spend time with your family." Angelina scolded.

Noelle laughed. "I just didn't want you to think…"

Angelina interrupted. "I know…I know…that you weren't pulling your weight. Blah blah blah blah blah! Now get! Besides here comes Brad now."

As she said that Noelle locked eyes with him as he was walking towards them from the barn.

"Hey," Brad said. "Everyone is in the house waiting for you. Those girls are excited and you had better hurry on in. I'll take care of these packages."

Noelle started to protest, "I can carry…

"Oh for goodness sakes, take these and get!" Angelina handed her a large pan of potatoes.

Noelle, with a tip of her head, said sweetly, "Thanks" as she headed into the house.

Angelina went back to unpacking when Brad interrupted her, "Do you think that we could take a walk before we go in. Will everything be okay for a little minute?"

Looking at her son, Angelina knew what conversation they were about to have. "Sure. Everything will be fine for a quick minute."

That being said she turned and Brad offered her his arm and they headed down the trail that took them to the back of the field.

"So…this is about Noelle, huh?

"How did you know?" Brad asked looking lovingly at the small framed woman beside him that had been both mother and father to two heart broken boys after they lost their dad.

"I've been watching you as you were puzzling your way through it. I take it you've come to some kind of a decision." Angelina said.

"It's been more about what God has been bringing me to. I had a talk with Genie this afternoon. I told her how I feel about Noelle and asked her permission to marry her daughter." Brad waited for his mother's reaction. Nothing came.

He stopped, so she stopped also. Looking at her he said, "No comment? That was a pretty big revelation for you to pass commenting on." Brad was watching.

"Honey, this is what I know about you. This is the biggest decision that you will make in your lifetime besides accepting God, not something to enter into lightly. You have been waiting all your maturing years to do this right. You wouldn't get to the finish line and mess up the race. You would finish strong. I would expect nothing less from you. If you feel that God is telling you this girl is the one, then I believe you. Is your heart involved? You're sure this isn't just a desire to help someone who's in need?" Angelina had to ask.

"I think that I have loved her since the moment that I rescued her from that car. There was this protective feeling that I couldn't explain and didn't understand until recently." Brad smiled.

"I think you have too. I also think that you will be a wonderful husband…just like your father was." Angelina squeezed her son's arm.

He kissed the top of her head. They walked a moment in silence, each one lost in their own thoughts.

"Well we knew this day would come. What next? I know you well enough to also know that you now have a plan." She laughed.

"I do. You do know me too well. Sunday I would like to take everyone to the park for a picnic. I'm going to ask her there. Because of the situation, I want to get married as quick as possible." He said.

"Exactly, what does 'as quick as possible' look like to you?" She asked.

Brad continued, "Sometime during this week while all of her family is here."

"That's quick…but is it possible? What if she says no, or what if she wants a big, flashy wedding. That would certainly take time." Angelina paused giving Brad time to respond to the questions.

He thought for only a moment, then answered, "She won't."

"To which question?"

"Both."

Brad, seeming very sure of himself, and in a very calm way said, "God is working all of this out.

135

Remember it is His idea. I am just following His lead.

"Okay, then what do you need from me?" Angelina waited for her son's reply.

"Nothing yet except one of your unbelievable picnic basket lunches." Brad answered quickly. "Let's get to Sunday and then we can all talk about what it looks like from there on. Okay?"

"Okay." Angelina answered.

They turned to walk back to the house.

"I have a ring." He smiled.

"You do?" She smiled too. She was surprised; but she shouldn't have been. Brad wouldn't do anything without being totally prepared.

"Are you going to let me see it?"

"Nope. I think she should be the first one to see it." Brad smiled. "But you can be the second."

"Good answer. Now let's get back and take care of our guest…our wedding guest."

****

In the house, the chatter was constant. The girls were all up on Noelle's bed. Her sisters wanted to hear everything that had been happening practically day by day for the last three months. Genie was content to just lie on the bed, listen to her girls laugh, and giggle together again. It was so clear to see how much they had missed each other.

Nissa was the first to say what they had all wanted to say. "Okay enough. I want to see the baby bump."

Anaya said, "Nissa!" Then she quickly laughed and added…Me too! Me too!

Noelle, seeming embarrassed, said all right. She

136

lifted up her shirt and lowered the waist of her pants. There was the firm, rounded bump that was the only telltale sign that she was pregnant, still small enough that her stretchy pants covered it nicely.

Both girls gently laid their hands on her belly and began to talk.

"Hi Baby!"

"Can you hear us? We can't wait to see you."

Genie sat up from her spot on the pillow and looking at her daughter asked, "May I?"

"Yes." Noelle looked at her mother and smiled.

Genie very gently ran her hand over the bump that represented the child that would be her first grandchild. "This is your grandma. I already love you. You are fearfully and wonderfully made. I speak life, love and joy over you. Blessings will follow you all the days of your life."

Noelle was tearing up as silence covered the room. No one wanted to move and break the spell.

Genie, removing her hand from Noelle's tummy, wiped a single tear from her cheek and then from Noelle's.

Nissa asked, "How can we love a baby so much that we don't even know?"

"I know." Anaya said. "Can you hardly wait to see the little face and feel it cuddle into your arms?"

Noelle's expression changed. She started to weep.

Genie wrapped her arms around her, "Oh Honey. It is going to be all right. God is working this all out."

"It's just that I'm so torn. On one hand, I don't want to miss a day of this miracle. Then I remind myself that if I attach and then decide that raising the baby isn't what's best for the baby, my heart is going to break even more." Noelle cried into her mother's arms. It felt so good. She just wanted to climb into those arms and let the world stay away for a while.

Anaya said, "Noelle, you aren't in this by yourself. We are family. We can all raise the baby. The important thing in the end is love."

"It's so important to have two parents." Noelle said.

"Really, how great did that work for us?" Nissa grunted.

Everything stopped in the room. They all looked at Nissa. She instantly realized that her comment was out of order. The comfortable silence of moments before became an uncomfortable silence.

Genie broke the awkward silence, "Girls, your dad was an important part of who you are today. What he did has not negated the role that he played as you grew. You loved him very much. Forgiveness doesn't look like bitterness."

"Sorry everyone." Nissa said.

"I know what you're saying though. I have these conversations back and forth with myself all of the time. Then I remember that I don't have to carry that burden and I give it back to God. Sometimes I just get down; then I take back the concerns and worries. I am working on trusting Him more. When I trust Him, everything goes smoother," Noelle shrugged.

"I know, most of the time anymore, I'm not so angry. The bitterness is certainly better than it was. I think that praying for him has been a huge help in getting out of the place that I was in." Nissa was honest with her feelings.

"Me too." Anaya added. "It used to be that the anger just ate me up inside and I was always stewing.

Now I think that I am beginning to feel sorry for him and all that he has lost. This may seem crazy, but the baby is one of the things that almost makes me feel sorry for him. He has a new generation in his lifeline coming that he will never know. His loss. Not ours. I refuse to look at this baby as a bad thing. I don't believe that any new life should enter the world with that burden. It is not as if the baby had a choice in any of this. All I know is that this baby is loved."

Noelle said, "I want to love this baby. But what if the baby is just a constant reminder of what happened to me?"

There it was, the elephant in the room, except no one seemed to see that as a problem but Noelle.

Genie rubbed soothingly up and down her daughter's arm as she said. "Noelle, we certainly don't mean to diminish what happened to you. Nor do we not understand what a horrendous act that was. But, do you know what brings me comfort when I think of that horrible night?"

"What?" Noelle asked.

"It's the fact that the drugs have wiped the memory of the ugliness of it from your mind. You do not have to have a visual remembrance of the abuse. Honey that is a blessing. Think of all of the women and children that live with those pictures buried deep in their mind every day. God was good and He protected you from that." Genie finished.

"I never really thought about it that way. I don't remember anything that happened. If God was going to protect me from something though, why didn't He protect me from everything?"

"He would have had to protect you from yourself. We have free will. You still made the choice to put yourself in harms way. Don't forget that we live in a fallen world. Remember that satan is here to kill, steal and destroy. He is not going to make it easy for us. We are called to be strong. It was our job as parents to prepare you for what you would face in the world. We failed in all of the ways of God." Genie said. "Now I'm trying to help you become a warrior in the midst of the battle. It's late…but with God, it is never too late. The four of us are learning together."

"I don't blame you Mom. I do accept responsibility for being there in the first place. I get all that you are saying about satan; then comes the questions. Do you know what bothers me the most?" Noelle said to the girls.

"What honey?" Genie asked, wanting so badly to stop the pain that her daughter was facing.

"I don't even know what my baby will look like?" She said.

Nissa and Anaya both jumped in yelling, "We do." "She," they paused for emphasis, "is going to look just like her mother. Beautiful."

They all laughed, and with that, the tough conversation was over.

✱✱✱✱✱✱✱✱✱✱✱✱✱✱✱✱

The day had turned out to be beautiful. They had walked out of the house that morning to the sound of birds singing and the sun peeking through the freshly opening leaves on the trees. Green grass was sprouting up and the dirty grey of winter's last had disappeared.

Noelle had loved going to church with her family and Brad's. It had felt so normal. The music had been great and the pastor's message was "Rebuilding after Trial or Tragedy." Noelle felt like God had master-minded the whole service just for her.

Brad had suggested on Saturday night that after church they should have lunch at the park. He had said that they couldn't possibly go back home without having one of Angelina's picnic lunches. She certainly had not let them down. The basket looked like it was prepared to serve a feast for kings and queens. There was country fried chicken, potato salad, homemade crescent rolls with Angelina's cherry jam, sweet potato chips and her canned dilly beans. The finishing touches were the homemade chocolate chip cookies and apple turnovers.

While the two moms got lunch all set up the girls went to the swings. Brad and Eyan came over and pushed all of them. Life felt careless. Noelle was basking in the love that was surrounding her. She noticed that there was peace flooding through her. All she could do was say, *Thank you God!*

"Come on everyone. Come eat." Angelina was calling.

They jumped off the swings and raced to the table. Nissa won. Noelle noticed that she had slowed and that Brad held back close by her in a very protective position. It reminded her of what she would live without because of her choices. There were so many little things that you don't think about that a husband would do for you. After all, they are programmed to protect; to be the warriors; the defenders of the home and family. Right? At church, the Pastor had talked about the position of the husband in the home. He talked about how God called the man to be the covering over his wife and children. He created him to be a shelter or a protector. That made her think about her dad. She started to go there, to that dark place where sorrow and sadness lurked. Instantly

141

she again recognized the dangerous path. She shivered as she realized that satan was again trying to snare her. Yet she was excited about the fact that he had no control over her. She said, "Get out satan. Go away. You can't draw me into your trap."

Brad looked at her, "What?"

"Oh sorry. Did I say that out loud?" Noelle laughed. "Sometimes I'm beginning to recognize the attacks of satan. I guess that God is developing a 'discerning spirit' in me. I was just telling him to get lost."

"Good for you." Brad nodded. "Let's eat."

When everyone was seated, Brad said "Shall we pray?" and as they all bowed their heads he said, *"Father, and most gracious God, thank You for bringing our two families together. We know that You never make mistakes and that everything that happens has a purpose. We are grateful for the bond that You are building between us and we look forward to the future and the path You are leading us. Bless us Father with Your presence, Your love and Your peace. We are totally devoted to You and anxiously wait to be in Your service. Bless this food to the nourishment of our bodies and build us strong for the jobs that You have for us to do. Keep satan at a distance and angels surrounding us. We love You. Amen.*

"Amen!" Everyone else emphasized.

Angelina said, "Let's eat."

And they ate. The food was, as always, amazing. That certainly was Angelina's gift. She could take anything and make it taste like no one else could. Even better than her cooking was the way that she made you feel, like there was no one more special for her to cook for than you.

They all ate until they could not possibly consider dessert yet, so they decided to have turnovers and cookies later. The girls spread a blanket and lay down with the sun warming them. In minutes, they were asleep.

Eyan talked the two mothers into playing a game of cards with him.

Brad took Noelle's hand and said, "Let's go for a walk."

"Okay." She answered. With her tummy full and the day as wonderful as it was, she could not image anything better than walking hand in hand with Brad Conroy.

Chapter Eleven

Psalm 96

Let the heavens rejoice,

let the earth be glad;

Let the sea resound,

and all that is in it;

NOELLE AND BRAD WALKED WITH A CARELESS-ness of two young adults who had not a problem in the world. The creation of God was all around them. They could see His handiwork in the beauty of the trees and the spring flowers. He was there in the birds in the air. They watched as squirrels ran tree-to-tree chasing each other. New life was everywhere that they looked.

Brad held her hand. There was a bonding between them. Noelle was enjoying his company. Not questioning; just being. What more could she ask?

Brad broke their silence, "Noelle are you happy?"

She looked at him tilting her head, "What do you mean?"

"I guess I mean could you do this always? If you had the choice, would you choose to walk in the woods with me or is there somewhere you would rather be? Is there something else that you would rather be doing? You know…if you had the choice?" He asked.

Noelle thought hard about his question. "If you're asking me where I would be besides right now, I can honestly say that there's no place that I could choose that would bring me more joy or peace than I have found right here."

"Why is that?" Brad continued to search her for answers.

"When my dad left, the peace that we found in our home was gone. We replaced it with the sadness of the situation. Mom did the best that she could to keep our home normal. However, we had to define a new normal. We all tried; but we didn't know how to do it. We didn't know how to let God rebuild our lives. It wasn't until we gave it all over to Him that I think any of us really began the healing process. We had been stuck in the sorrow. In our pain, we were erecting walls of despair. The walls were becoming so high we were not going to be able to scale them so they were becoming our own prisons. The anger and bitterness were beginning to define us and we were making decisions based on those negative attitudes. We had just surrendered into those feelings. Not having God to help us through the heartbreak, we weren't equipped to fight back. We were helpless to ward off the attacks of satan. We became defenseless and just surrendered. It has only been since accepting Jesus and studying His word that we are building ourselves up strong enough to recognize His direction. We have all started

praying for our dad. It was not an easy thing for us to do; but if we hadn't we weren't going to be able to begin the healing process. We all struggle with unanswered questions. By letting God lead us down the path of healing, He can bring us the answers that we need when we need them. We may never understand the whys...but we can understand that it wasn't our fault and that we have a Father who loves us and will never leave us."

She continued, thinking aloud as she walked and talked. "Change didn't just happen inside of our home, it happened outside also. The town became a gossip pool so that even school was no longer a safe place. We had been the family that everyone wanted. I learned that it made people feel better about their problems to find out that we were not as perfect as we looked. Up until then, my life just felt like life. I didn't know that it could be any different. We associated with people who had the same means that we had. The people with problems were just the families that my mom did her volunteer work to help. They didn't really affect me. Now I see where the pity that I had for other people in their struggles should have been sympathy. I should have had more compassion for the challenges that they were facing instead of just feeling sorry for them and thankful that it didn't affect me."

"So, when it all fell apart and I moved to campus, for me the college life was an escape. It was totally new and I was going to try the other side of life; after all, the way that I was raised had just become a lie."

"What I didn't know was that what I was looking for wasn't something that I was going to find in any place or through any people. I needed that personal relationship with my Savior. He needed to be my real daddy."

"I learned that here. I have learned what real love looks like. Don't get me wrong. Before Dad left, our home was full of love. That was the shock. After he was gone, Mom did everything that she could to keep that love growing. But, she was even more broken than we were! She had just lost the love of her life. Her life was completely undefined for the first time ever. As a couple, there had always been a plan that they had been working towards all of their married life. Then with the stroke of a pen, the plan was gone and so was Dad. It was such a surprise ending. There were never fights between them, no distance or separation. To watch them, they looked like they were still on their honeymoon. Dad appeared to adore her. To all of us around them they looked like they had the perfect marriage." She finished.

Brad watched as the expression on her face changed. He could tell that she was really thinking.

147

"After all that you have been through, are you afraid of marriage?" He asked.

Noelle shook her head, "I don't think so. In fact, I think that it has opened my eyes to the importance of building that foundation on Jesus Christ. I learned that we couldn't foolproof anything on our own. I think that if God ever allows me the opportunity to have love and family with marriage, what I have learned will make me a better wife and mother. I don't think that He would allow me to walk through this without being able to use it. You know what I mean?"

"I know just what you mean." Brad said.

He continued. "So what you're saying is that you want marriage and a husband to build a life with. I also hear you saying you want an enormous house full of tons of children running around screaming and yelling." With that last statement, Brad emphasized enormous with his hands letting go of Noelle's hand as he did so and making sure that he grasped it again.

"I don't think that I said any of that. I am positive I did not say tons of children. And I know that I didn't say anything about them screaming and yelling."

As she started to laugh, Brad raised her hand to his lips and gently kissed it. Noelle was always surprised at the times that Brad would show her affection. She was never sure what he was thinking during those moments or why he would do it. She knew that she liked it when he did.

They continued walking in silence with the sun breaking through onto them periodically. They were comfortable with the silence. These were moments that Noelle would cherish in the days to come when she would find herself lonely and facing tough decisions.

The two of them had just come to a clearing in

the woods with a little bench. Brad, without taking his eyes off her, lowered her hand and said, "Why don't we sit?"

Turning to her Brad noticed the confusion on her face and said, "Noelle, don't ever be scared of me. I would never hurt you. I would lay down my life to protect you."

"I know. I'm not scared." She answered still so unsure of what was happening.

"I need you to understand a few things and I don't want to do anything that makes you uncomfortable or unsure of me. So…if I say anything that makes you want to run, just say so and I'll stop. Okay?"

"Okay." Noelle nodded her head hesitantly.

Brad nodded back and collecting his words he said, "I've waited for God to send the girl to me that would be the perfect partner for me for life. Understand what I'm saying. I'm a 'for life' kind of guy. It's all or nothing. I'll never leave my family. Never. Do you understand what I'm saying? I'm not your dad. I'm a sticker. I won't go away. No matter what comes in life. Okay?" He was speaking slowly and waiting for her to understand all that he was saying. He waited for her to answer.

"Okay…I think I understand. You're not my dad."

"I really need you to hear what I am saying Noelle. I think that I have loved you from the moment that I first saw you. There you sat, broken, in that car, a mess. And just as spunky as anyone that I've ever seen. In that moment, in me, welled up an intense desire to fix all that was breaking in you, to protect you from whatever had hurt you. I wanted to get you out of that car and hold you so that the world could not ever hurt

149

you again. I just knew that you would be safe in my arms. It was a desire that I did not even understand. All that I knew was that I had to make everything in your world all better. I have prayed that some how God would right your world. Then the confusion stopped as God dropped into my spirit the understanding of what was going on. I was in love. For the first time in my life, I was getting what it felt like to have the love that a man feels for a woman. I began to ask God to guide and direct our relationship and I believe that He has. He has reassured me that He is in control and I promise you that I have not made a move without His nudge. I've also asked Him to prepare you for this moment."

"What moment?" She asked. Brad could hear the confusion in her voice.

"This moment my sweet girl." Brad smiled as he gently tucked a loose strand of hair behind her ear.

Noelle was sure that her stomach was tied in a knot. She felt like she had to tell her body to take a breath. Breathing was something that it was supposed to do voluntarily; yet, it did not seem to be able to do that.

Brad reached into the pocket of his shorts. As he did, he got down on one knee. Taking Noelle's hand in his and looking deep into her soul he asked, "Noelle Smith will you marry me? Will you come along side of me for life as we build a family together? Will you work with me, play with me, and grow old with me? I love you, now and forever. Together we will raise this baby in a home that will teach the love of the Lord. Then, when the time is right, we will give him or her brothers and sisters. We will build a family with God as our foundation. Will you do that with me? Will you love me? Will you let me protect you; be your provider and help nurture you into the woman that God created

150

you to be? I promise that I will never hold you back and that I will embrace that determined spirit of yours. I will love you more everyday that God blesses us with life. When death separates us, we will know that we have been loved more than anyone else could have ever loved us. I will be there for you and I will never leave you except that God take me away. Grow old with me. Go with me where God takes us and build a future with me. Be the woman who stands by my side, be my encourager and my lover. Be my best friend, my perfect fit. Be the woman that God created just for me. Can you do that? Will you trust me enough to take my hand and walk into the future with me? Will you marry me?"

Noelle could not believe what she was hearing. She could not even see the ring that was in the box. Her eyes were filled with tears. She was in shock.

Brad asked, "Noelle, can I put this ring on your finger?"

Noelle could not speak. Looking straight into the eyes of the most wonderful man that she had ever met, she nodded her head yes. She couldn't stop looking at this man who was offering her life, abundant life. Just like what God had said that He had for her. Brad was offering her life above and beyond anything that she could have imagined.

Brad slipped the ring onto her finger and kissed it. "When we stand before the Lord and become man and wife, then I'll kiss you the way that I want to right now. I'll honor you now and I'll honor you forever."

Brad came up onto the bench and as he sat beside Noelle, he stretched his arm around her back. She looked at the man who had just offered her his life. Noelle laid her head into the crook of his arm. He could feel the tremors of her body as she cried.

He heard her softly say, "I never thought."

"I know; but God loves you and so do I. I won't ever get tired of telling you." He laid his head on her head and they just sat, in the quiet of the woods, wrapped in the creation of God's world, with the music of the birds singing as the heavens rejoiced, Brad began to pray.

"Thank You God. Thank You for all that You've done and are going to do. We will serve You all the days of our lives. We ask that You will pour out Your blessing on our life, our marriage and our baby. From this day forward, this marriage will be built on the foundation of Your word and we will teach it to our children. Give me the strength to lead as a man of God. Help me to build the family that belongs to You; the family that You have so graciously trusted into my earthly care. I promise Father to continue to grow closer to You so that I will be the man that You have called to this task. "As for me and my house…we will serve the Lord." Your Word will be upon our lips; praise to you will be a daily occurrence and prayer will be our love language. We offer ourselves as a daily sacrifice. Use us however You see fit. We will trust You all the days of our lives. Thank you for Your love. Amen.

After praying, Brad reached over and with his eyes asked Noelle if he could. She nodded her head. He carefully placed his hand on her abdomen saying, "Hi my baby. I am going to be the best daddy that you could ever have. With God's help your mommy and I are going to take good care of you."

The tears just continued to fall from Noelle's eyes. How could she have been so blessed? She would never stop telling God thank you for as long as she lived.

Brad reached into his pocket and pulled out his

hankie. As he handed it to Noelle he asked, "Is this going to become a common practice?" He chuckled. "Should I collect a larger supply of hankies? Why is it that the male, who rarely cries, is the one who carries the hankie for the female who weeps at the slightest tug on her heart?"

Noelle wiped her eyes and blew her nose. "Did you not just tell me that you would take care of me?"

"Yes I did you little woman urchin." He answered as he tipped her nose.

She handed him back the hankie and smiled, "Then carry my hankie please."

He chuckled as he nodded his head and took back the used hankie, "To the ends of the earth My Lady."

They just continued to sit snuggled close together and basking in the reality of what had just happened and what was going to be happening. Time had no bearing on their life right now. They were just two people enjoying each other in the music of God's natural symphony. The beauty around them that was bringing them such joy could not compare to the joy that was bursting into Noelle's spirit. She was loved. She was loved by a man of God who wanted to understand who she was created to be. Noelle knew that he would help her discover the secrets of God for her life. He would be a guide in helping her to learn about her creator and she would be his helpmate. Someone who he could depend on to be his cheerleader; to support him through thick and thin and to walk this life with him as he had said, "till death do them part." There would be no good-bye letter. Noelle knew deep in her heart that the love that he had for the Lord would not allow that to ever happen. She would work at being a great wife. She would never want this man to feel like he had made a mistake. She would honor him always.

The world stood still for the two of them as they continued to rest in the assurance of who they were.

"Brad?"

"Yes Noelle."

"What does our future look like?" Noelle wondered.

"I thought that I already covered that. Huge house, tons of kids, lots of noise." He smiled at her.

She gave him that look, "No really do you have a plan?"

Chuckling aloud he answered, "When you know me as well as my mom knows me, you'll know that I always have a plan. I have been thinking this through. However, you are more than welcome to have a better idea. I am open to conversation; but this is what I've been thinking. Do you want to hear it?" He paused.

"Yes...please?"

"We're four months away from having a baby. I would like to get married as quickly as possible. Your mom and sisters are here right now. My thought is that we get married while they're here." He waited and gave her time to process his suggestion.

Looking at him she said, "They're only here until next weekend."

"Right."

"Right? You mean that you want to marry me within the next five or six days?"

"No."

"Okay. I thought that's what you were saying." She seemed relieved.

"I'm saying that I want...to marry you today. But, I think...that we should get married Thursday or

154

Friday or at the latest Saturday. Before they go back home?"

She looked at him assured that she would find this all to be a joke. She did not see any sign that confirmed that.

"How?" She asked.

"Well…first let me ask this question. Do you want a large wedding? I mean, I understand if you do. Little girls always dream of their wedding day don't they? You know, big poufy dresses, lots of flowers and hoopla; a day where you are the princess. Is that what you want? If it is…I'll make that happen." He waited for her answer and could tell that she was deep in thought.

"No. I don't feel like that's important to me. It may have been years ago; but my life has changed so much. I think that I put importance on different things now." She answered with all sincerity.

Brad searched her face carefully trying to make sure that she was not surrendering important dreams because of the situation. He did not see that in her expression at all.

"I don't need a big whoopla to take this step with you. In fact, I think that I would want it very small and intimate, my family, your family and maybe some of the people from the restaurant. I think that I would like to have my Aunt Debbie here though. She has always been an important part of our life. I think I would feel like the day would be missing something without her."

"Then Aunt Debbie it is." He smiled.

"But even small, how do we make it happen so quickly. Are you thinking that we'll go to the Justice of Peace and be married at the Court House?" She asked.

"No. We should have a wedding before God and loved ones. Not just a ceremony." He looked puzzled

155

like he wasn't sure if he should suggest his next thought.

"Come on tell me, what are you thinking?" She nudged his ribs.

"Well, what if we brought our minister into the restaurant. Decorated one of the formal rooms with lots of lights and candles and did everything there. I want you to know it is okay to say no if you think it's a bad idea." He said.

She squealed, "I love it. That is a perfect idea. I love the restaurant. But when and how do we do that without causing your mom a lot of problems."

"I doubt that will be the issue. I'm willing to wage that Mom will jump at the idea. She loves stuff like this."

"Yes, but, this is her celebration to enjoy too. How is that going to happen if she's working so hard? I don't know if that's a good idea for us to cause her more stress."

Brad loved that she was so concerned for someone else at a time like this. "Let's just throw it out there. If she doesn't immediately love the idea, then we'll go to plan B."

"Which is?" Noelle asked

"Punt."

Laughing she said, "Okay…I trust you."

"Awesome. But do you love me?" Brad asked very seriously.

Noelle raised her hand and lovingly touched the side of his face, "I'm learning what love really is. I've had feelings for you also from the start that I tried not to claim. I didn't think that anyone could ever love me with the mess that I've made in my life, especially someone as special as you. I don't want to casually say those words. Can I have time to soak in all that's happened? I promise you this; that I will respect you. I promise that I will stand beside you. I promise to take care of you. And I promise you that when I say those words they will come from my heart and you will know that they will be forever. Is that enough for right now? I know that you deserve so much more."

Brad pulled her hand to his lips and gently kissed each finger as he said, "It's worth waiting for. I know that your love will be worth waiting for."

Noelle began to cry again as she watched the tenderness that Brad showed her.

He very affectionately wiped the tears away saying, "Now stop crying before I have to pull out your handkerchief again.

She laughed.

"So tell me if you like your ring."

Noelle realized that she hadn't really seen the ring. The tears of before had blurred her vision. Taking her first look, she gasped. "It's beautiful. Oh Brad...I love it." The princess cut diamond sparkled in the sun on her petite finger.

"Oh sure, that's just like a girl. Love the diamond but not the guy."

Looking into his eyes and hoping that he could feel the words straight into his soul, "I couldn't be more blessed. Thank you for being you." She kissed his cheek letting her lips linger and feeling the promise of a future.

Enjoying their alone time for just a little while longer, they prepared to meet the family and share their news.

"I wonder what my mom will say?" Noelle pondered.

"She said yes." Brad answered.

"What? She knows?"

"Yup. I had to ask her permission. She loves me. I could tell." Noelle wrinkled her nose at him.

"And your mom?"

"Yup. She loves me too."

"You know what I mean." Noelle playfully jabbed him in his side.

"They're on our team. My mom already knew. She reads me like a book. Your mom cried, must run in the family. Do you think I should start carrying more than one hankie? Maybe I should carry two. Or what about your sisters, do I need to carry their's until I walk them down the aisle and hand over the hankie to their husbands?" Brad thought himself quite cleaver.

That earned him another loving jab to the ribs, "And my sisters? Do they approve? I can't believe that they could keep this secret." Noelle said.

"Now they don't know and neither does my brother. I probably would have told him; but with him coming here from the camp that he has been working at this week, I didn't have any time alone with him. Besides you should get to tell someone don't you think?"

"It sounds like you're doing a fine job of telling, Mr. Conroy. I will gladly stand by your side while you break the news. My job should be to flash this rock that you just put on my finger." Noelle raised her hand letting the sparkle from the diamond dance around them.

"Okay then...if you're ready let's go. Let the planning begin."

Standing, he offered her his hand. She stood and he pulled her close, "To the future Mrs. Conroy. Could I hold you just for a minute?"

"Please do Mr. Conroy."

As he softly cuddled her close, laying her head

against his chest, she could hear the rush of his heart beating. It felt as if it was in rhythm with hers.

"Brad?"

"What my sweet one?"

"Don't ever let go…okay?"

"Never. I promise."

As they walked back holding hands, all eyes were on them. Eyan had taken over the pushing job at the swing set. Seeing the couple coming back holding hands, everything stopped. Noelle took a mental picture and tucked it away in the recesses of her mind. It was a memory that she wanted to keep forever. By the time that they had reached the picnic table, both of their moms were crying. His brother and her sisters came running over. The moms were sharing a big hug.

"Would someone like to tell us what's going on?" Eyan asked.

"Yaahhh? The girls chimed in together.

Noelle looked at Brad giving him the nod and He said as she flashed her hand, "She said yes."

The moms cheered and the three siblings were speechless, all echoing at the same time, "What?"

Brad made explanations that he had fallen head over heals in love with Noelle. He said, "I asked her to marry me and she's said that she will. In the mean time she's going to work on learning how to love me."

That was the showstopper. You could have heard a pin drop.

"Okay. Just kidding. She loves me. Who wouldn't?"

The girls came running to Noelle hugging and

dancing around in a circle.

Eyan slapped Brad's back and said, "What took you so long? I knew from the first night. The look in your eyes told me that you fell hard. Remember?"

Brad laughed, "I do. God leads me a little slower than He leads you. I had to give her a little time to figure out what a great catch I was."

"You are a great catch and I love you Bro. There is nothing more that I want for you than for you to be happy and madly in love with this beautiful girl. The best part is that she is just as beautiful in her spirit. You are going to have a great life." Eyan said as he pulled him into a huge bear hug. "Seriously…I am so happy for you."

"Happy enough to be my best man?"

"Forever…I'll be that guy forever. I will always have your back."

Brad and Eyan enjoyed their time while allowing the girls this time to embrace their moment.

Chapter Twelve

Psalm 96

Let the fields be

jubilant,

and everything in them.

Then all the trees of the

f orest will sing for joy;

THE WEEK HAD BEEN A BLUR. WHEN BRAD THREW out the suggestion that they do the wedding at the restaurant, Angelina was instantly so excited she could hardly stand it.

Before they had time to sit down at the picnic table, the ideas were already being thrown around. They all agreed that Friday was a great day for a wedding.

Always the cook, Angelina thought that they should serve their choice steaks from the ranch with a second option of chicken breast smothered in a white cream sauce. The chicken would be served on rice. The beef would be accompanied with baby red potatoes in an Italian marinade. There would be green beans with toasted almonds. Completing the menu would be a fresh green salad mix with lots of vegetables. Of course, wedding cake with ice cream on the side would finish out the night.

Although Angelina offered to make the cake, Noelle said no. Noelle knew Angelina well enough to know that she would have so many great ideas that she would never stop working right up to the time that Noelle was walking toward her groom. "I don't want you to have to spend your whole week working. I would much rather have you go with us to look for dresses."

She was so touched to be included in such a precious moment that she gave up making the cake without a fuss.

Angelina decided that they would close the restaurant all day on Friday. There was a little shop in town that not only would make the cake; but, they also would come in and do all of the decorations. They would ask the restaurant staff to do the cooking and help "The Sweet Shoppe" with all of the preparations. That would free the families to focus on getting themselves ready. Angelina insisted that Noelle was going to take the week off to get ready and to spend this precious time with her mom and sisters. At first, Noelle was adamant that she could not do that to Angelina. However, as they began to make of list of all that would need to be done, she finally surrendered. She was getting married in five days. Five days. In just five days, she would be Mrs. Bradley Conroy. The name of her father would be replaced in her life as his presence had been by the love of her heavenly father. He would not be here to physically walk her down the aisle and place her hand into the anxious man at the end of the church aisle. The dreams of little girl wishes would be put aside as her future loomed before her. Noelle had to pause and remind herself that different was not always bad. Different could be exciting and adventurous. It could be filled with love, respect, and a hope of the best to come. Different did not have to feel like the pain of rejection. Not today. Today different looked like love.

Brad watched his bride's expression change and he knew that she had taken a bunny path somewhere that had caused her to pause.

Standing at the end of the table, reality sank in and she laughed aloud, "Oh, my gosh...I'm getting married in five days."

Brad, coming around to where she was standing, grabbed her, and swinging her round and round said, "We are getting married in five days!"

Everyone clapped and cheered.

✳✳✳✳✳✳✳✳✳✳✳✳✳✳✳✳

Monday rolled around and the first item on the

list was the visit to the doctor's office for the ultra sound. It was decided that not only would Noelle's mom and sisters be going, but so would Brad.

As Noelle talked to her mom the night before, she expressed, "I'm a little embarrassed having Brad come with us. They will have to expose my stomach to do this. We haven't even kissed yet."

"Honey, this is a time of bonding with the life that's growing inside of you. Brad deserves the opportunity to hear that baby's heart beat and see the life that God created just for the two of you. It is very clear that he loves you very much. He would never put you into a situation where you were uncomfortable. If he knew that you were unsure about him being there, I am sure that he would understand. However, I think that you would be depriving him of an opportunity that he will never have again. Would you feel better if the girls and I didn't go?"

"No Mom. I want you there. I'm sure it will be fine. It's just me. I'm probably being a little sensitive. This is all happening so fast. I have to adjust so quickly to so many things." Noelle said.

"You do want to marry Brad, right?" Genie studied her daughter intently.

"Yes. Absolutely." She smiled just at the thought of him. "God has given me a gift that I never expected to have. Brad has all of the qualities of an excellent husband and father. I have watched the way he responds to his mother. The way that he has treated me from the very beginning tells me he is a man of integrity and honor. I know that he loves me. I don't know why. He could have chosen someone without baggage." Noelle touched her tummy where life was growing inside of her. "No, I know that he loves me."

165

Frowning Genie ventured again, "Do I hear a but?"

"Not about getting married; just about...well... what if I'm not good enough for him? What if I can't do this right? I don't want to fail him. And don't think that I blame you; but I'm one of the statistics. I'm a product of a failed marriage. What if...."

"Stop it right there. You are not going to carry the stigma of a statistic. You are a born again creation. All things are new and old things have passed away. No more do any of us walk in the remnants of that old life. We are going to take the good and leave the bad. This is a fresh start. We are not going back. We're moving ahead." Adamantly she emphasized that last statement.

Noelle, getting teary, grabbed ahold of her mother, "I love you so much. Thank you for being who you are. If I can only be half the mother that you've been, my baby will have a great life."

"You just never forget that you live under the 'new covenant' not the 'old'. Your dad and I did not know about the blood of Jesus. We did not understand the ramifications of a life without Him, or heaven, or hell. We didn't understand about His love for us."

Genie grabbed her daughter by the shoulders and drawing her close she said, "The world labels Noelle, not God. Throw those old thoughts away, and rise up oh daughter of the risen King." She whispered these words of comfort into her daughter's ear as she held her tight. Genie loved the feel of her daughter in her arms. Her mind raced through the years, seeing Noelle tiny and dependent, watching, as she grew defiant and exploring; and now coming out of brokenness. She was getting stronger everyday. Thank you God.

****

The doctor's office was not that large. It felt like an army had just invaded the premises. There were only enough seats for the girls. Brad leaned against the wall beside a chair for Noelle who had gone to the window to check in.

"Are all of these people with you?" The elderly receptionist asked cautiously.

"Yes, first baby." She sheepishly answered.

"Well the room is small; but I suppose that the tech can squeeze everybody in.

"Thank you." Noelle turned and sat down beside Brad as she started to answer all of the questions that were on the sheets regarding her medical history.

Brad saw her hesitate, as she had to check the "single" box. He could tell that she was embarrassed. Leaning forward he whispered in her ear, "It'll all get better by the end of the week."

"Promise?"

"I promise. We're going to be okay." She loved the calming effect that his presence had on her.

"I believe you."

"Noelle?" The door had opened and an older woman called her name. "I hear we have a group?"

"Yes. We are a little eager." Brad answered.

They were ushered into the hall where the pre-liminary steps were taken. On the scale she went. Blood pressure and pulse monitored; pleasantries exchanged. Everything was very professional. The medical assistant asked them to follow her and she took them to a back room with a table, a rolling stool and one extra chair.

On her way out of the room, before closing

the door she said, "The room is pretty small. Make yourselves at home and our tech will be here in a moment."

Noelle sat on the table and Brad positioned himself discretely to the backside of the table. Genie sat down in the chair and the girls lined themselves up against the wall. The two of them were chattering away. Their excitement was over flowing.

Genie was watching Brad. She saw the intuitive way that he seemed to sense Noelle's unease. He sweetly rubbed her back in a soothing way and she could see her daughter relaxing.

The door opened and in came a rather large, jovial man. "I heard you're all having a baby and I thought that I'd stop by and take a few pictures."

Genie watched Noelle's reaction to having another man enter the room. The technician didn't miss a beat.

"This room gets small enough when I walk in, but you all make it seem like a closet. It's going to get hot in here when we start having some fun. My name's Jermaine and I'll be your server today. I'm about to serve you up one beautiful baby." He said.

Instantly the atmosphere in the room became energized. Noelle relaxed and was soon swept away on the wave of excitement.

"Now little momma, you lay back here and let's get some of this cold, sticky goo on that tummy. I'm willing to bet that we're about to hear the most amazing sound that you've ever heard."

Noelle lay back with the help of Brad. The tech raised her shirt up discretely and rolled the waist of her stretch pants down. Squirting the clear jell onto her tummy, Noelle jumped. Brad patted her shoulder.

"I told you it was cold." He laughed as he began to slide the probe slowly across her tummy. All eyes were on the monitor and the room became so quiet you couldn't even hear breathing.

"Oh boy here we go." Jermaine said. "Listen." He turned a button on the machine and a whooshing filled the air, loud and fast.

"Whoosh, whoosh, whoosh, whoosh, whoosh." The baby became real; heart beating, life changing, real.

Brad reached down and squeezed Noelle's hand. She looked into his eyes and they both knew this was the defining moment that cemented them. "That's our baby." He smiled.

Her heart welled up with emotion. All she could do was nod.

"Lookie here; we have blast off. Let me introduce you. Family…that is your baby." Jermaine began circling on the monitor. There is our baby's head." Then a moment later, "That is one fine looking leg. Are we looking to know boy or girl?" He asked.

Instantly they looked at each other and smiled. Together they said, "No."

"No?" Jermaine questioned.

"No." They reaffirmed.

"What?" Nissa and Anaya practically shouted at the same time.

"No. There are so few good surprises in this world any more. This is a really good one. When the baby is born Brad can have that moment of coming to the waiting room and making the announcement." Noelle said.

Brad squeezed her hand again, as if to say "thank you." He felt like he had been given a gift.

Noelle smiled back with her silent "you are

welcome." It excited her that he was pleased.

"Well if it will make it any easier for you girls, this baby is modest and is covering up by crossing its legs. He or she is going to hold that secret anyway. Must be planning on a big entrance. Or else we have a stubborn baby here."

"Just like her mother." Brad teased.

"Her? The girls picked up on his use of the f emale pronoun.

"Yup. Daddy's little girl." He winked at Noelle. She blushed.

Everyone continued to watch as Jermaine took pictures and checked through his list of duties.

"Well everything looks great to me." He proclaimed handing the printed pictures to Noelle.

"Can you show me one more time what I'm looking at?" Noelle asked.

Grabbing a marker, he began to circle and label body parts. "Yes sir, this is one beautiful little girl." They all looked at him. "…Or boy." He chuckled.

Noelle's sisters groaned with disappointment. The anticipation might seem like a great idea to Brad and Noelle; but Nissa and Anaya thought that four months seemed like a lifetime. They weren't sure how they would be able to endure until then.

It was decided that Genie and the girls would leave the two of them alone to meet the doctor. Genie had suggested to the girls ahead of time that Noelle might be more at ease answering the questions that Genie anticipated might be coming. After watching the calming affect that Brad had on Noelle, she was glad that he would be in the room with Noelle at that point. They all kissed her and left the room to go and wait in the reception area.

"Well Momma…I have to say that will always rate as one of the most amazing moments in my life. I just experienced my first child's heartbeat."

"That was pretty unreal. Just think that we could actually hear life flowing through the baby and still in my tummy. Incredible. I'm in awe."

Brad took hold of her hand and kissed her fingers one at a time. "Thank you for this gift. Thank you for trusting me enough to let me come."

"I'm glad you were here. I don't know how I could have ever explained to you what that felt like. There just are not words. However, I do have to say that you seem sure that this little one is a girl. You know, he may be hearing you say that. You should be careful that you don't make him feel bad." She teased.

"You think I'm kidding. I'm not. I'm telling you that we are having a girl. And she is going to love me."

Laughing Noelle answered, "You think everybody loves you." She teased. "I would have to agree that if you are right…yes…she will."

The door opened and a very serious middle-aged woman in a long white medical coat walked in. She extended her hand first to Noelle and then to Brad. "I'm Dr. Smiley and I am one of the doctors in this practice. There are three of us. Normally we would make sure that you see all of us at some point before giving birth; however, due to the late start of your appointment schedule I can't promise you that will be possible. All that I can tell you is that we will do our best. If it doesn't happen rest assured that we are all quite capable and each will do their best to ensure that a healthy mommy and baby are the outcome of this experience."

As she finished with her introduction, Dr. Smiley, which later Brad and Noelle would agree the name certainly did not fit the personality, began to ask questions.

"May I call you Noelle?" She asked.

"Yes."

"Noelle, normally we see a new mother earlier than 20 weeks. So let's go back and get some important history updated before we continue. Is there a reason why we are not seeing you before this time?"

"Well…" Noelle hesitated to answer as she stumbled over her words.

"Dr. Smiley, call me Brad. He offered her his hand, giving her a strng shake. Noelle just moved here from Atlanta, Georgia. She hasn't been in the area very long."

"I see…did you see a doctor there Noelle?"

"No."

"Okay. May I just speed this process up by being blunt?"

"Yes."

"Brad, are you the father?

"I am now. Noelle and I are going to be married on Friday. Listen…let me just help you out here. What Noelle is struggling to tell you is that she was date raped in Georgia and a pregnancy ensued. She came here. We fell in love and we are going to be married. The rape was her first encounter with a man. She has had a lot to adjust to and accept. She is working through all of that. What we are here for is to make sure that everything is progressing as it should be and we too are looking for a healthy mommy, healthy baby at delivery."

You could have cut the tension in the room with a knife. Dr. Smiley silently continued looking at the file in front of her for some time. Then putting down her pen and file said, "I assume that I came off too professional and not so very compassionate. I do apologize. I cannot assume to understand what you have experienced. So let's start again. This is what I want you to know. All women who are pregnant, married or not, are given the same blood work. All are checked for sexually transmitted diseases. You will receive nothing more than you would have received in a normal situation. We are always very thorough. The blood work will be drawn today and we will have results quickly. I see no reason to anticipate or prepare for a problem unless we were to find that there was one. The office would call you if that were the case and we would have that discussion then. For now, I am more concerned about getting you started on pre-natal vitamins…

Noelle interrupted, "I have been taking them since I went to the clinic when I thought something was wrong. They did the pregnancy check and gave me pre-natal vitamins then."

Dr. Smiley seemed happy to know that. "Excellent. Then I suggest that we finish a discussion on your medical history and then you can schedule your next appointment for four weeks. However, I would like you to schedule a sugar test with the lab for sometime in the next couple of weeks."

From that point on the appointment seemed to flow more easily. Noelle could not have been more thankful that Brad had been there to handle the earlier discussion. He always had such a calming approach.

The doctor offered Noelle a hand to help her sit up on the table. She was preparing to leave as she turned and asked, "Are there any questions that I may answer for you before I leave?"

Noelle started to say "no."

However, Brad did have a question and he felt

it was a question that was the most important. "Yes, I do. We are Christians and our faith is very important to us. All decisions that we make in our life are made to reflect that walk. It is important for us to know that we have yoked to people who understand the importance of Jesus Christ in our lives. After all, we would not want to have an emergency and then discover that we were not of like belief. So if I may be so bold, Dr. Smiley, are you a believer?"

For the first time Dr. Smiley did just that, she smiled. "I guess I had better work on the love of the Lord reflecting more in my everyday walk, Brad. Yes, I am a believer and I try to base my decisions in life, as in crises, on His principles. I truly am sorry. I feel like I have given the two of you a very wrong picture of who I am. Thank you for your boldness. It is refreshing to see some one so young not ashamed of our Savior. Not an excuse, but sometimes the challenges of daily life can cause us to forget our true mission. Our office is here to serve you. If you have any questions before your next check up feel free to call. We will do all that we can to answer them." Stepping forward she shook both of their hands and said, "Congratulations! You are going to have a baby." With that, she left the room.

Brad could almost feel the tension in Noelle leave as Dr. Smiley closed the door. "Well she wouldn't be our first choice. However, God uses every experience to His glory. Maybe He just used us as a reminder to her today. Let's see what next month brings."

"You'll be here with me won't you?" Noelle asked.

"You couldn't drag me away." He answered kissing the top of her head. Let's go. We have a wedding to prepare for.

****

The plan was that Angelina would be meeting them for lunch at a restaurant near the mall in downtown Indianapolis. They had all tried their best to get her to come with them to the ultrasound. Angelina had insisted that she needed to go into the restaurant and start the plans for Friday. She needed to get an order in and fill in the staff. They needed to start the arrangements for the restaurant to close on Friday.

She did seem very excited about all that there was to do. "Thank you so much for offering; how about I just meet you for lunch?" She asked.

They arranged to meet for lunch. After lunch, Brad would swap vehicles with his mom and he would head home while all the girls went dress shopping.

Across from the restaurant, was a gift store. They placed their orders and Brad excused himself saying that he would be right back. On his return, he handed Noelle a gift bag and asked, "Want to open it?"

Noelle was learning this about her future husband; he loved to give gifts as much if not more than he liked receiving them. He was as excited about her opening the package as she was. Noelle untied the ribbon that held the bag closed. Removing the tissue paper and reaching inside she pulled a three-picture frame out that said, "Baby's First Pictures." Under the frame was a matching photo album with the same words, embossed across the front. Everyone at the table oohed and aahed as Noelle traced the little green frogs and yellow butterflies that covered the gifts.

Noelle smiled at Brad as he said, "Little girls like frogs too!"

"Yes they do." She giggled. "Thank you for being so thoughtful." She reached across the table and squeezed his hand.

Raising her hand, he kissed it and staring into her eyes he slowly answered, "You're more than welcome."

The rest of the table quieted, watching the interaction between the two. They felt like they were infringing on a private moment; but could not pull their eyes from the sweet moment of affection that was happening in front of them. Nissa and Anaya were almost drooling. They thought Brad was the most thoughtful man alive and they were so happy for Noelle.

Angelina winked at Genie and the two moms shared their own moment of private communication. They both knew that their babies were going to be just fine.

✶✶✶✶✶✶✶✶✶✶✶✶✶✶✶✶

Brad left the women to their shopping. He was not invited. This was girl time. Besides, he had his own mission. First, he had to stop at the school and arrange for time off this week and then he was off to purchase a wedding gift for his new bride.

His professors were very happy for him and set up his assignments to accommodate for the few days that he would be missing.

Next, he knew just what he was looking for and right where he would head to buy Noelle's gift. There was an Amish furniture store off the beaten path on the way home. He would have plenty of time to accomplish his mission and get home, tucking the gift away in the barn where no one would look for it before he gave it to her. He was so excited. This was a lot of fun. No wonder God loved to give His children gifts.

Angelina took the girls into the big mall to a store that carried formal wears. They were looking for Noelle's dress first and then they would decide what the rest of them would wear. Noelle went into the fitting room and they began to bring dresses to her. She tried each of them on and they looked nice but not perfect. Leaving the fitting room, she went onto the floor and began to look through the racks and racks of dresses. There were so many choices that it was almost over-whelming.

Noelle had been through three racks of dresses and was about to give up when she saw it. There it was. Seeing the dress that she knew would be her dress, she took it back to the room and slipped into it. Turning in front of the mirror, she smiled at the picture that looked back at her.

"Noelle," her Mom called. "Are you in there?"

Noelle opened the door and stepped out and onto the raised mini floor stage in the center of the fitting room doors.

Watching her mom's reaction confirmed what Noelle already knew. She had found the dress. It was a narrow shoulder strap with a fitted "V" cut bodice, empire waist and A-line skirt. There was a chiffon overlay. It was simple and flowing. Turning she showed her mother the back. Deep "V" cut with a small train.

"Beautiful. Simple and elegant." Was all that Genie said. "You are going to make a beautiful bride. I can't wait to see Brad's face." A single tear slipped down her cheek.

"Oh Mom, I am so happy." Noelle replied.

"I know Honey. I know. I am so happy for you. You are going to have a wonderful life with Brad." Genie

177

hugged her tight.

Angelina and the girls had made their way over watching the emotion that was playing out in front of them. The dress was beautiful and all agreed that this was Noelle's dress.

They were off to a good start; now on to the rest of the wedding party. As they had been browsing through the dresses, the sisters had found a color that they all really liked and decided that it was perfect. Noelle's sisters would wear the soft melon color and they found a similar cut dress to Noelle's, in a three quarter length. The girls loved the dress. Time to beautify the moms. It was agreed that Genie and Angelina would wear the same dress, but in a deeper shade. Angelina objected at first saying that the mother of the bride should stand out more.

Noelle insisted, "We are marrying our two families together. You both are giving away your children so to speak. Besides this is my wedding and I can do anything that I want, right?"

Genie stepped in and said, "I would love to share this dress with you. I think it's a perfect idea."

Angelina was touched beyond words.

Noelle's dress was the only one that needed any alterations. The woman doing the alterations promised that the dress would be ready on Wednesday. Off to the shoe store and then jewelry. They were all having so much fun they did not want to stop.

After a full afternoon of girl time with purchases made Noelle said, "Well, I think that we're done."

"Not quite yet." Her mother smiled. "Follow us."

They were all giggling as they led Noelle through the mall with a purpose. Reaching an "intimate apparel" boutique and turning to face Noelle, Genie said, "A bride cannot go to her new bride groom with out preparing herself. You are a gift. We have to wrap you up.

"Mom!" Noelle blushed.

"Come on. This is going to be fun." Then Nissa and Anaya charged ahead.

Soon enough, Noelle forgot about her embarrass-ment and began to have the best time. She walked out carry a bag of several new items. However, the ultimate purchase was a long, flowing white gown, tastefully beautiful. That was what her sisters thought when they saw her holding it up. Now they could go home.

That ended their very busy and productive Monday. Brad was out in the barn when they ar-rived at home. They tucked away their packages and went into the kitchen to help Angelina prepare a quick supper. After having a big lunch, they decided that soup and sandwiches would be plenty before bedtime.

Eyan was coming in just as they were putting the meal on the table.

"Hi Honey. How was your day?" Angelina smiled at her youngest son.

"Great." He replied grabbing a chip out of the bowl that Nissa was carrying. She slapped his hand playfully. Eyan pulled back as if having been mortally wounded. "So, I talked to Pastor Travis today about officiating on Friday. He was really excited; but he would like to meet with Brad and Noelle before." Travis Gates had been the boys' youth pastor all through their growing up years. He knew them about as well as anyone. Noelle, he had not really met yet. "I told him that I would have Brad call him tomorrow."

"Thanks Honey. Of course, he would want to meet with them. Thank you for taking care of that. In the business of this day, we totally forgot about making those arrangements. We had too many other important things to do, like buying dresses, shoes and jewelry."

"Oh right. Way more important than seeing that there was someone to make Friday legal."

Brad walked in during that conversation and walking over to Noelle gave her a quick hug. "Speaking about legal, tomorrow we have to go to the courthouse and apply for the marriage license. I think that we have to have three days before the wedding. I had a scary thought today though. We have to bring a copy of our Birth Certificates. Do you have yours?"

Brad's question brought everyone to a pause. They all turned and looked at Noelle.

"I do have it. When I left, I took any important papers that I thought I might need. Relax. The wedding is still on." Noelle chuckled at the way everyone panicked.

With his arm around her shoulders, he gave her a little shake. "Look at my wife-to-be; such a little planner."

"Speaking of planning...we were planning on going into town tomorrow anyway and making arrangements for a few flowers. We could go by the courthouse first, if that works with your schedule?" Noelle offered.

"Well unless you have a preference about flowers, I took the liberty of stopping while I was out today and I placed an order for everything that we should need. I also stopped and talked with them at the Sweet Shoppe and I arranged for them to be at the restaurant with the cake at 2:00 p.m. I had the flowers delivered there at the same time. I ordered the cake to match the flowers and told them that Mom would be getting a hold of them to talk about how she wanted the room set up. I hope that's okay. I'm not trying to make decisions without your input. I was just thinking about time and I didn't know if you would need another day to find your dresses. I wanted to make sure we didn't have a last minute rush."

Everyone laughed to think that Brad didn't think that planning a wedding in five days was a last minute rush.

"No that's great. Anything that you choose will be perfect. That was so thoughtful of you to do that. Thank you." Noelle smiled letting him know that she really was pleased with his forethought."

"Great. Then tomorrow we can go to the courthouse and take care of everything there and we should be set. "

"Set as soon as you give Travis a call and schedule some one on one time for you and Noelle." Eyan injected.

"Done...I'll do that tonight."

"Wait." Angelina said, "We haven't decided what you guys are going to wear.

"We took care of that today too. Eyan and I are the same size. We talked about it and decided to rent tuxedos. I stopped in today and they measured me for both of us. We just went classic black with white shirt, black tie and black vest. I told them if the bride had a different idea we would call tomorrow. What do you think?"

"I think that my groom will be very handsome."

"That's my girl." He kissed the top of her head.

They all loved watching the play of affection between the two people that they loved so much.

"Okay then we'll eat. Eyan, do you want to

pray?" Angelina suggested as she took the hands of those on each side of her. Everyone else followed suit as Eyan bowed his head.

"Wait!" Brad interjected. Jumping up from the table and grabbing the frame on the snack bar where it had been lovingly positioned he said, "Look at this beauty" as he held up his picture of the baby's ultrasound to Eyan. This is her head and this is an arm. These are her legs crossed; she's very modest."

"Wow. That is the cutest looking alien that I have ever seen." Eyan exaggerated his enthusiasm. "She... we are having a girl?"

"Well she didn't let us know that...but I know that." Brad answered.

Eyan just laughed at his brother.

Noelle watched the interaction between the two brothers. She couldn't miss the pride that Brad exhibited as he showed off his picture. The emotion of that moment stuck in her throat as her eyes blurred.

Brad said, "It is time to pray. We all have so much to be thankful for."

"Then let's do it," Eyan took the lead.

Our Father in heaven, hallowed be Your name. Your kingdom come, Your will be done on earth as it is in heaven. Give us today our daily bread. Forgive us our debts, as we also have forgiven our debtors. And lead us not into temptation, but deliver us from the evil one. For Thine is the kingdom, and the power, and the glory, forever and ever and ever. Thank you Father for all that you have masterminded. Thank you for the joining of these two families and for the blessed future that we are all going to have. We pray for continued development of our beautiful baby. That he, (laughingly clearing his throat and pausing) or she...will grow strong in Your ways and that all of his...or...her days will be lived in Your blessing and under Your protective covering. Be with each of us as we prepare for Friday, and may everything that happens reflect how much we as a family love You. Amen and amen.

"Let's eat!"

Chapter Thirteen

Psalm 96:13

They will sing before the LORD,

for He comes,

He comes to judge the earth.

He will judge the world in righteousness

and the people in His truth.

THE SUN WAS SWAYING ACROSS THE BEDROOM IN A dance of grace and beauty as if playing tag with the leaves of the trees. Noelle moved and stretched, the fogginess of her still slumbering mind slowly woke to the reality of what today was. Today was her wedding day. She was getting married. By the end of the night, she would be Mrs. Bradley Conroy. In less than four short months, she had run away from her home in search of an abortion. She had reached the lowest point in her life. God's hand had directed her to this amazing family where Angelina had literally been a lifeline. Her child lived and the oldest son was asking her to spend the rest of her life building a home and family with him.

Unbelievable! Noelle thought to herself. That was a lot of life in a short period. It felt to her as if time had stood still to allow these changes to happen so quickly. Yet there was no fear. She knew that God was still on the throne and He was planning every step that they were taking. She knew that she would walk into the unknown with Brad.

She had slept hard last night. The rush of this week's activities had kept her mind from thinking about the changes that again were happening to her. Her thoughts traveled to the man who was going to become her husband at the end of this day. In spite of everything, she was in amazement at the way that God had orchestrated this union. Noelle was still working on accepting that she was worthy of such a man as Brad Conroy. His patient love for her was more than she could comprehend. The fact that he could see value in her still left her in awe. When her mind would travel to that train of thought, she would remind herself that

God loved her and saw her as white as snow. She tried to remember that the only person who did not was the person who looked back at her from the mirror. She was the self-condemning party, not Brad and not God. Brad treated her as a prize. He let her know daily how precious she was to him.

Self-esteem had never been an area of struggle for her; if she was truthful with herself, she probably had a pumped up view of who she was. This last year had been a very humbling experience. Seeing faults in her personality was part of the positive that had come from her life change. She was finding a new compassion for people and the struggles that they were going through. One of the questions that Pastor Travis had asked her in their marriage counseling was, "What positive has come through the trial that you have walked through?" Her immediate answer had been, "Brad." Rebecca, his wife, had laughed at her and said, "That is too easy an answer." Noelle asked if she could think about that for a while.

She had pondered that question the last couple of days. She had even asked God to lead her in a specific direction. God being so faithful had done just that. He had shown her the selfishness that used to permeate her everyday life. Now she was developing better listening skills and trying to see the real pain of the people that she talked to everyday at the restaurant. She realized how many times she would ask, "How are you?" and then never really care how they were. Noelle now was careful to hear their answer and try to understand their needs. Sometimes it was no more than a friendly ear, a warm smile or a compassionate word. She was learning that people need people. We were created for relationships; first with our Heavenly Father and then with other people. This was not an easy transformation

186

for Noelle to make.

She ventured into her own wounds, many that she had no control over. The wounds created by her father, who was supposed to love her, and then by her friends, who had gossiped about her, had left her guarded and closed off. It was Angelina and her family and their love for teaching the love of Christ that was bringing her walls down piece by piece. She was truly learning how to love. She had learned it is easy to love when life is comfortable. It is harder to love when people come with flaws and live in their wounds. Wounds cause people to develop traits that are not always so pretty. She was beginning to see through the coping skills that people use, sarcasm, bitterness, silence, anger, frustration, short fuses. Noelle was recognizing that these are all emotions that push others away and cause distance. When what they really need is true love, warmth and understanding. She recognized them easier now after her walk through her own valley. Her answer today would be that the positive that was coming out of this was a more compassionate heart and a better recognition of where people were and what they needed. She was learning how to love through Christ's heart and not her own broken one.

She journeyed back to Wednesday, when she and Brad had met with Pastor Travis and his wife Rebecca. He was a middle-aged man, who as a youth pastor, still seemed relevant to the teenagers of today. He explained after introducing Rebecca that he liked to do marriage counseling as a couple. "My wife completes me and brings a woman's perspective into our conversations. She will understand from your perspective things that God did not create me to get. His wife was fun and full of life, a complete compliment to the calm of his personality. The passion they have for this generation of youth is evident in all that they say and do. Noelle had not had conversation with them before this meeting. She liked them right away. It was clear that he had great respect for the family that she was marrying into, and a special bond with Brad and Eyan. It was just as clear that they respected and loved this man. Noelle could tell that he had filled a portion of the role that their father would have filled had he lived. Noelle also knew, from everything that she had seen as she spent day-to-day life with the brothers that their father would have been so proud of the young men that they had become. Her heart swelled when she thought of the influence that they were going to be in helping to raise the child that she carried.

As she had talked with Pastor Travis, he did not ask for her whole story; but before the night was over, she found herself telling everything that had happened to her; from her father leaving, to the night of the rape. She then shared her amazement at finding herself at the Conroy house. It seemed easier every time that she told it. Not that she intended to tell it often. Somehow, it just seemed right sharing with the Pastor and his wife. Noelle was sure that they would play an important role in the life that Brad and she would build together. She did not feel condemnation, just compassion. Brad let her tell her story as the two men sat quiet, intently listening. Rebecca wiped tears from her eyes. Noelle had not even noticed that tears fell from her own. The weight of the pain that she carries seemed lighter as she finished. Travis asked only one question when she was done. "Have you forgiven your dad and the young "men" who did this to you?"

The room was silent as Noelle answered honestly, "I'm trying to. I know the importance of forgiveness and the bitterness and strife that unforgiveness can bring. It is certainly easier to forgive knowing that if I had not come down this road, I would not have found Brad. But I can't tell you what I would feel if I were to come face to face with either my dad or the men who violated me."

"I would recommend strongly that you search inwardly for that answer. I can promise you, that if you do not lay that demon to rest, it will surely rear its ugly head in the future. That isn't something that you want to take with you into this union."

Noelle agreed that she needed to find that true forgiveness. She did not want satan to have any area of her life.

They talked about what they knew about each other, both agreeing that they had so much to learn. Pastor thought that under the circumstances, it would be a good idea that after the wedding they continue to meet for a few weeks. He usually walked with his couples through a series of studies. Even though they would already be married, he felt it would be very beneficial. He wanted to make sure that they were starting on the right foot. They agreed to call at the end of next week and set up a regular time to meet weekly.

Pastor asked them what they thought the ceremony should look like. Both agreed that they wanted a very traditional service. It would be small and intimate and based on love. Rebecca brightened the mood by offering to sing. Lovingly Pastor Travis reached over and taking his wife's hand said, "Perhaps another time Honey." Noelle missed the joke and Brad had to interject that the only time she was allowed to sing was when she did her unique version of "Happy Birthday". Otherwise, they left the singing to others.

189

They had a good laugh at Rebecca's expense, who did not seem to mind at all.

Noelle said, "I've been reading the Book of Ruth. As short as it is, I think that it speaks volumes. Here are three women who have lost their husbands to death. Ruth releases her daughter-in-laws to leave her and return to their own families. One decides to go. Ruth is an example of the reflection of God's love and devotion. Ruth's complete devotion to the Israelite family who took her into their family and made her one of their own shows such love from both sides. Then when Naomi tries to send her back, to release her to find a new life, I loved what Ruth said. "Don't urge me to leave you or to turn back from you. Where you go, I will go and where you stay, I will stay. Your people will be my people and your God my God."

"I love that Naomi finds blessings through the kindness of Ruth and Boaz. She really exemplified the truth of the coming Kingdom of God and that participation in His Kingdom will not be decided by blood and birth; but by how we conform to the will of God through obedience to Him through faith."

"I was that foreigner in an unknown land. I saw God through Angelina's obedience to Him by living out her faith walk daily. Out of that, our families are going to join in a love walk that changes my families' lives forever. I see myself in the pages of Ruth's story. I see my future. It looks very different than it could have."

Pastor Travis agreed that the story was a perfect way to join their lives together and he said that he would try to tell it as beautifully as Noelle had just done. Noelle seemed embarrassed at his words of kindness; yet looking at Brad she could see the look of pride that he was wearing for his coming bride. She would cherish this look all the days of their life. That look made her feel as if she had found her home.

Noelle hung onto that memory as she stored it in the recesses of her mind so that she could draw upon it for years to come. She knew that she never wanted to do anything that would dim that look in his eyes. She wanted to be the wife that brought those emotions in him to the surface. Noelle wanted Brad to respect her and feel that moment of pride all the days that God gave them together.

Just then, as she was enjoying the fond walk through that day, there was a knock on the bedroom door and it drew her from her roaming thoughts. Straightening up the bed covers and running her fingers through her hair she answered, "Come in."

Opening the door part way, Brad poked his head in with a big smile saying, "I brought my wife-to-be breakfast in bed? Is that all right?"

"Only if you promise that this is going to become a habit."

"Today I will promise you anything. Reality is I'll keep it only for special occasions. Otherwise you'll get bored with my gesture."

She giggled, "I promise that I'll never tire of your kindness, Mr. Conroy. Come in and show me what you've brought me."

The smell of the covered tray was intriguing to say the least. Noelle could not wait to see what was hiding under it.

"What's that smell? It smells too good to eat." She uncovered the tray and there were two plates of Eggs Benedict with rye toast and a fresh bowl of fruit for them to share.

"Hold that thought." Brad said as he settled the

tray on her lap and headed for the door. In he came with a large bouquet of flowers on a tray with two glasses of orange juice. "I couldn't carry two trays. I had to make two trips. Actually…I made many trips. I brought breakfast for your family too, not quite as fancy as ours; but this is our day. Right? Plus mom makes it look easier than it really is." He sat the tray down removing the flowers and placing them on the dresser so that she could enjoy them.

"I got four other vases of flowers for all the rest of our ladies. I want them to feel special today too. I put them outside their bedroom doors with a card telling them how much I look forward to building a relationship with them. Corny, huh?"

"Sweet…It is one of the special characteristics that I love about you. You have a desire to care about others. Not only do you think about others first; but it matters to you if they feel special."

Noelle could see that he was uncomfortable with the praise that she was giving him. She smiled as he said, "I thought that maybe we could start this day off with prayer and breakfast."

"I'd like that." Noelle bowed her head.

Heavenly Father, Creator of all things, Maker of heaven and earth, we come to you today and we covet your blessings on our life. We ask Father that you will bless us with love. Love for You and love for each other. We ask that as we find a home, You will fill it with children who will also walk in Your ways. Please pour out Your favor of blessings on Noelle and I and all of our descendants. Seal our marriage with Your protective hand and lead us in wisdom in all decisions that we have to make. May this day be a day that makes You smile and may You fill it up with memories to last us a lifetime? We are forever Yours. Amen.

Brad kissed Noelle's cheek, "Boy…it's a good thing that we didn't have a long time to wait for our wedding night. I want to kiss you so bad that I can hardly wait until tonight."

"What if I'm a bad kisser?" Noelle teased.

"Then practice makes perfect. We'll practice a lot. Now eat up. We're going to need our strength."

Noelle, tasting the meal that her to-be-husband had made, was amazed. "Well cooking is certainly in your genes. This is awesome. You can cook for me anytime that you want."

"You couldn't live around my mom very long without picking up a few tricks. Mom used the holidays to teach us kitchen skills. The tradition was Eyan and I had to go through the cookbooks and choose a dish that we wanted to make. She would take us to the store, we would buy the ingredients and she would help us make it. That was our contribution to the holiday meals. It got us off to a great start in the kitchen. Funny thing was Eyan always wanted to make the same thing. He had to make a dish we called mud. It had a cookie crust and different puddings with gummy worms sticking out of the whipped cream. It was his favorite and became a holiday classic at our table."

While they ate, they talked of lighter things. Brad discussed with her an offer that Angelina had made last night.

"Mom has thrown a suggestion out for us to consider. She is suggesting that until we decide what we want to do about housing, she will move into my bedroom downstairs and we will move into hers. Her room up here is large with its own connecting bathroom. We would have plenty of room to put the baby in this room. It would be convenient for the baby to have a room with her own bathroom. And we could have the whole upstairs to ourselves."

"With *her* own bathroom? Really?" Noelle tried to look scolding.

"That's what I said." Brad stood firm. He was so sure that the baby was a girl.

"Besides, we couldn't put your mom out of her own room." Again, Noelle was surprised by the generosity of the woman who was to become her moth-er-in-law in just a few hours.

"Well, the room that I'm in was actually Mom and Dad's room. After Dad died, Mom decided that she should move Eyan and me downstairs and she should move up. There are two bedrooms downstairs, each with a bathroom. The truth is, she just could not stand the thought of sleeping in the room that they shared all by herself. It has worked all these years. My room is bigger than all of the rooms upstairs and it is closer to the kitchen, which is where Mom really loves to be. Listen it's up to you. We can look for a place of our own or we can take her up on her offer and take some time to get our bearings. We've made a lot of decisions in a short period of time." He left the conversation wide open trying to feel her out.

"If you're sure that it's okay with your mother, it's fine with me. I love it here; but I will go anywhere you go. As long as we're together, we'll be fine." Brad knew that Noelle was telling him exactly how she felt. His future wife had a face that hid nothing.

"Okay. I will let Mom know. She left for the restaurant early. Her car was gone before light. She left us a note telling all of us to enjoy our day and that she would be back as soon as she saw that the cake and flowers had arrived."

"I feel so lazy doing nothing while she's working so hard."

"Stop it. Today is your day. I'm sure that you will more than make up for these days off. I am a little afraid that I'm marrying my mother. I'm thinking that I might just be trading one workaholic for another."

Noelle knew that Brad was teasing her; however, she had really missed the restaurant this week while she was off. Since working there, she had discovered that she loved meeting the people and offering them a time of service, hopefully brightening their day. She understood totally, why Angelina loved what she did. Noelle was going back as soon as this weekend was over.

As they finished the wonderful meal that Brad had fixed he stood up and said, "Okay…I'm going to leave you to yourself. The next time that I see you, I'll be waiting for you to come down the aisle and marry me."

Noelle smiled; he knew there was no aisle at the restaurant. However, that did not matter. Today she was marrying the man who loved her. And the emotions that stirred in her let her know that the feelings were becoming mutual. She could not wait to tell him. She had been asking God to give her a spirit of love for her husband. Again, God being God was faithful. Noelle could feel the stirrings every time that she was around Brad. There was a need to be with him that was becoming so strong that she knew she was falling deeply in love with the man who was to be her life mate. For now, she would keep that little secret tucked away in her heart.

"Thank you for breakfast. Now I won't be wasting away from hunger when you see me."

"For better or worse. I'm just planning for better." On that note, he took the trays and dishes and started for the kitchen. Turning he said, "Oh...I almost forgot. I have a present for my bride. Close your eyes."

"You do? But I don't have one for you." She answered with a sad look on her face.

Putting down the trays, he smiled at her and said, "You are my present. Now close your eyes."

Noelle did as she was told. She could hear noises; but she did not peek.

"Okay you can open your eyes." Brad said.

In front of her was the most beautiful wooden, oak, glider rocker. It was a perfect honey color. There was a country designed upholstered cushion on the seat and up the back.

"Oh Brad. It's wonderful. Thank you." She said as she jumped out of bed and sat down loving the feel as she glided back and forth.

"Your welcome. I can't wait to see you rocking our baby off to sleep. That will be my gift." With that said, he picked up the trays and walked out the door closing it softly behind him.

Father I am the luckiest woman on earth. Thank you! And thank you for answering my prayers. I can't wait to belong to Brad.

She hardly had the prayer off her lips when the door flew open and in came Nissa and Anaya yelling, "You're getting married today and he's wonderful. He gave us flowers."

She laughed at their enthusiasm.

The morning flew by with hot soaking tubs and doing each other's nails and hair. Genie enjoyed every minute with her girls; treasuring these moments, knowing that at the end of the day they would be going into yet another phase. She was not ready to give her daughter away. Gale should have been here. He should have walked her to the man that professes his love for her. Gale should have handed their daughter's hand to Brad and gently kissed her cheek, saying, in a way that only a father could, "I love you." However, that was not going to happen. Today would look like their new normal and for now, she would not waste one more minute thinking about what could have been, but savoring what was. She would love her daughters.

By the time that Angelina got home, they were all ready except for putting on their dresses, which they would do at the restaurant. It gave them the opportunity to focus all of their attention on the woman who had made them feel so much like a part of her family.

After having a nice hot bath, Angelina went, as commanded, to Noelle's room where she was given the works, facial, hair and nails. There she enjoyed a real treat of girl talk; something that Angelina had never been accustomed to. She loved being included in these precious moments with this family. She knew what a gift they were giving her by asking that she be a part of their last day as family as they knew it. She expressed her gratitude more than once.

"We…are family now, all of us. God has brought us together. And together we'll stay." Genie said as she looked into the mirror at the woman looking back at her. The girls all came and gathered around Angelina sitting in the chair.

After a long group hug, they heard, "Thank you… all of you. You've made this day as special for me as I hope it will be for all of you." Smiling she said, "Now no crying," and she wiped the start of a tear away." Laughing she
197

continued, "Or we will ruin our makeup.

Laughing they all agreed.

After hours of preparation, the time had come to make the drive to the restaurant and slip into their dresses.

They loaded up into two cars. Nissa went with Angelina, jumping into the SUV that had all of their dresses. Noelle and Anaya slid into Genie's car with her driving and off they went.

It did not take them long to get ready once they were there. Noelle was surprised to find there was a photographer waiting for them. She was snapping pictures and capturing the memories of the day. Lisa was one of their regular diners and when she saw they were closing the restaurant for the wedding, she insisted they allow her to take pictures for them. Angelina was thrilled to know this pleased Noelle. This was Angelina's gift to these two precious people in her life. Angelina thought it was important for everyone to look at where they started so they could realize how far they had come.

When they arrived at the restaurant, Lisa had already snapped pictures of Brad and Eyan. Then as they were getting dressed, she was snapping pictures of the girls, with a few posed shots of the finished product.

They laughed, hugged, and savored the moment. Noelle tucked every look, every feeling, and every sound away in the recesses of her mind. She was living in the moment. She did not want to forget one precious minute of this day. She would cherish these moments for a lifetime. Just a short time ago, she did not even know if she would see her family again and now here they all were sharing the day a girl dreams about. This day she would walk to the man who waits with love in his eyes for only her. Today she felt like a princess and she would never forget how her life had changed through the love of a God who loved her that much.

"Hey!" Eyan knocked on the door to the room.

"Who is it?" Noelle asked.

"Eyan."

"Come in." She replied.

Opening the door, Eyan popped his head in and gave a loud wolf whistle. "Wow, nice job. You all clean up really well."

Nissa and Anaya both whistled back. Nissa commented, "You're not so bad for a country boy yourself?" Eyan did a quick spin as he entered the room with flair. "I've been sent to see if we're ready. There's a man out there on pins and needles waiting for a beautiful woman to join him."

Noelle blushed. Tucking another moment away she said, "You tell him I'm more than ready. Why don't you take our moms with you and get everybody situated. The girls and I will come right behind you.

"You got it boss. Hey...just so you know...I'm glad that you're the one." Saying that he blew her a kiss. Eyan then kissed the cheeks of each of the mom's, stepped forward and offered them his arms. "Let's do what the lady said."

As they started to leave, Genie paused. Turning and looking back, she moved to hug her daughter. Not able to speak, she just smiled, stroked her cheek and turned back to her position on Eyan's arm. Off they went. Genie thought, the next time that I see Noelle it will be through the eyes of my son-in-law.

"Are we ready?" Noelle turned to Nissa and Anaya and saw the tears in their eyes. "Now stop it or we'll look like raccoons with mascara smearing around our eyes."

Noelle, escorted by a sister on each side, left the room. She could hear music playing and recognized the song that they had sung at church a few weeks ago. She had commented to Brad that she thought it was beautiful. The song was "Draw Me Close To You." Again, she marveled at the man whom she was marrying, the man who never seemed to miss a beat. Even a small detail like making sure that she had music for her wedding and that the song was something that she had said she liked to him in passing. She determined that she would spend forever trying to make him as happy as he made her.

As they entered the room, it took her breath away. Brad had filled the room with flowers and candles. The candles created an aisle that led her to the man of her dreams. She felt like she was floating to her destiny. This man would encourage her to soar. He would help her to be the best that she could possibly be. She would learn to love God and him with all that was in her.

As they started down the aisle, Nissa and Anaya paused and kissed their sister's cheek; they stepped back and allowed Noelle her entrance.

Noelle's mind took a picture of the look on Brad's face as she came down the aisle that he built for her. Reaching Brad, the girls stayed back and she stepped forward taking the same hand that had reached out to her like a lifeline in her darkest moment.

"You're beautiful." He said.

"Thank you…for everything." She answered.

Pastor Travis' words resounded with wisdom and love.

I Corinthians 13
Love is patient, love is kind. It does not envy, it does

*not boast, it is not proud. It is not rude, it is not self-
seeking, it is not easily angered, it keeps no record of
wrongs. Love does not delight in evil but rejoices with
the truth. It always protects, always trusts, always
hopes, always perseveres. Love never fails.*

Pastor continued, "During our marriage
counseling session, Noelle shared this beautiful story
from Ruth. He recapped the words as best he could the
way that Noelle had shared them. "Ruth is an example
of the reflection of God's love and devotion. Ruth's
complete devotion to the Israelite family who took her
into their family and made her one of their own shows
such love from both sides. Then when Naomi tries to
send her back, to release her to find a new life, Noelle
loved what Ruth said. "Don't urge me to leave you or to
turn back from you. Where you go, I will go and where
you stay, I will stay. Your people will be my people and
your God my God."

Noelle loved that Naomi finds blessings through
the kindness of Ruth and Boaz. She really exemplified the truth of the coming Kingdom of God and that
participation in His Kingdom will not be decided by
blood and birth; but by how we conform to the will
of God through obedience to Him through faith. Our
acceptance in His Kingdom was determined by
accepting Jesus Christ as our Savior and was sealed by
the shedding of His blood on the cross. Nothing can
separate us from His love." Pastor finished with, "I could
not have said it better myself.

As Noelle stood holding hands and facing Brad,
their mothers and family, formed a circle around them.
It showed a bond of protection, a picture of the two
families uniting. Noelle and Brad stood in the center.

Pastor Travis and Rebecca holding hands gently laid their hands on the young couple's shoulders standing in front of them. Pastor Travis asked everyone surrounding them to join hands and they made a circle signifying the protective covering of God love. With friends looking on they made vows to love, cherish and obey until death do them part.

Brad took a paper from his pocket and began to read Genesis 2:21:

The man said,

"This is now bone of my bones and flesh of my flesh; she shall be called 'woman,' for she was taken out of man." For this reason a man will leave his father and mother and be united to his wife, and they will become one flesh."

He continued, Malachi also talks of the marriage union.

Malachi 2:15 Has not the LORD, made them one? In flesh and spirit they are His. And why one? Because He was seeking Godly offspring. So guard yourself in your spirit, and do not break faith with the wife of your youth.

"Noelle, I promise that all my days I will obey God's commandments. I will be by your side until death do us part. I will remain faithful to the covenant that we have promised to one another and to God this day. I will be your protector and provider, your friend and companion. Together we will raise up our children in the ways of the Lord."

At this Brad smiled and with a wink said to her, "All ten loud little rug rats." Everyone laughed; but only the two of them knew why.

"All of our children will be the culmination of our union and our love. We will raise them in the love and admonition of the Lord. We will be His people and He will be our God. Noelle, you are my wife. God has given you to me and in everything that we do, we will always be one."

With that vowed, Brad placed the ring on Noelle's hand and bending his head, he kissed the ring on her tiny finger sealing it with his love.

Noelle was not sure that she would be able to continue. Brad's words had touched her deeply. Not only had he made sure that she understood that he was with her for life; but he had also made sure that she knew this baby was theirs.

Looking to Brad for strength, her confidence grew as he smiled at her and nodded his head giving her a wink for confidence.

"Brad, you are my future. Through the love of God on that first day, your persistence saved me from myself. Today I take a vow to be your helpmate. I am making a decision to choose to serve you for the rest of my life. I will cherish your love and honor you all of our days. As did Ruth, I make this vow to you. "Don't urge me to leave you or to turn back from you. Where you go, I will go and where you stay, I will stay. Your people will be my people and your God my God. Brad I will stand by your side forevermore." With tears gently sliding down her cheeks, Noelle placed the ring on Brad's finger and following his lead, gently kissed the ring.

After the exchange of rings, Pastor said, "In the name of Jesus Christ and in the presence of these witnesses, I now pronounce you husband and wife. You may now kiss your bride."

Brad raised the netting that covered the beautiful face that he would wake up to every morning. This was the woman who would share his dreams and his sorrows.

203

She would raise their children with him and together they would build a family that loved Jesus.

Taking Noelle's face in his hands, he slowly moved closer, there was no need to hurry. They had a lifetime. First, he gently kissed the tears that had fallen from her eyes. Then ever so slowly he pressed his lips to hers, he kissed her with a love that was forever. Taking his time and savoring the feel of this closeness, he knew that God had blessed his patience. Finally pulling back and looking deep into the eyes that swallowed him up he said, "I love you Mrs. Conroy."

Smiling back into those eyes of emotion, Noelle answered, "I do...love you too Mr. Conroy."

Brad's heart soared. His dream had come true. God had been so faithful. Thank you God for all that You have done.

No one moved allowing the two people before them this moment of privacy. This was a time to seal, "what God had brought together and no man could separate."

Pastor said, "Let's pray."

Heavenly Father, today in Your presence we thank you for the lives that You have brought together. We ask Your protective covering be over this new family. We thank You that they will walk in Your blessings and that they have made decisions to serve you all the days of their lives. We ask that those days be long, that they be happy and that they be fruitful. In Jesus Name. AMEN.

One more kiss and then the joy of sharing this union with everyone else. The couple received the hugs, kisses, and shouts of joy. There were well wishes from family first and then the friends from the restaurant. Noelle felt like the luckiest woman on the face of the earth. Then she saw her Aunt Debbie. She could not have asked for more. Noelle started to cry as her Aunt grabbed hold of her and, hugging her said, "There is nothing that could change the love that I have for you. We are family and will always be. We are on the same team."

"Thank you. I wanted you to be here so bad." Noelle said looking into those eyes that looked so much like her own.

Taking her face into her hands she said, "You're welcome. There is no place on this earth that I would rather be. You are my special girl. I was there when you were born and I'll be there as long as God allows me." Then she kissed her cheek.

Noelle could not have been happier. She felt like she should pinch herself to make sure this wasn't a dream. But her dream just continued. With everyone circling around, Brad announced, "I am going to dance our first dance together with my lovely bride." Eyan started the music one more time. As "Draw Me Close" began to play again, and the guests stepped back creating a space for dancing, Brad took Noelle into his arms and swayed with her to the rhythm of the music as they created a memory to hold in her heart forever. Never could she have imagined being so cherished.

The music ended and he kissed her another time whispering into her ear, "I'll never tire of kissing you. I've waited a lifetime to feel your lips."

"These lips were made for you." Noelle smiled into the eyes that held her close, "You can kiss me anytime that you want."

The people called for them to kiss again…and they did, repeatedly.

Laughing Brad addressed the people that were

there because they loved them so much. "Thank you for sharing this day with us. We would not have it any other way. We hope that you know how much we love you and how much you mean to us; that being said, let's pray and eat.

"Most Gracious God, thank you for bringing us together. Pour Your favor out on Your children. We love You. Bless all those who are here today and keep us all moving closer to You daily. Now bless this food and the hands that have provided and prepared it. In Jesus name. Amen."

The bride and groom moved to the tables where the food was set up and everyone else followed.

After a time of visiting with everyone there, opening gifts and again saying thank you, Brad surprised Noelle with the news that they were going away for a few days.

"Where? What about clothes?"

"Our destination is a surprise. The suitcases are packed. I had your mom and sisters take care of all of that. However, they will be gone when we get back so you will have to say goodbye now. I'm sorry they have to leave before we return."

"Shhhh!" Noelle placed her finger up against Brad's lips until he stopped talking. She kissed him and said, "I belong to you now. I'll go where you go."

"You are my precious gift and I promise to treasure you forever." Brad responded with another kiss.

Noelle turned to her mom. Grabbing her she said, "I love you Mom. I wish you were going to be here when I get back. Thank you for everything. For loving me even when all looked like I had totally screwed up my life."

"You're my baby girl. I could not do anything

but love you. Have a wonderful time. Make it magic." She kissed her little girl good-bye releasing her into womanhood.

Saying good-bye to Nissa and Anaya was not as easy. They were already crying before she hugged them. "It's going to be okay. We can only be separated by distance. Our hearts will always be connected. I love you both more than you'll ever know." With that, she hugged them one last time.

Brad had already said his good-byes to his mom and brother. Noelle turned to Angelina and said, "I can never thank you enough for sharing yourself with me. You saved our baby and started a future generation. I already love you. Thank you...Mom."

Angelina, pulling her close, squeezed, as tightly as she could; then quickly let go saying, "Go. Soar."

Eyan grabbed a quick hug. "See you in a few days, Sis." Noelle tapped his cheek.

Cheering started as they headed for the door. Then stopping, Noelle took her bouquet and tossed it behind her. Her sisters jumped but it flew over their heads and landed purposefully into Michelle's hands. Taking her by surprise, Michelle grabbed the flowers and waved them at Noelle as she and Brad hurried out the door to start their life as man and wife.

Thoughts

From

The

Author

I HOPE THAT ALL OF YOU HAVE ENJOYED THE TIME YOU'VE spent journeying with Noelle, Brad and their families. You have been a part of their history as they have begun a walk that will continue through two more books.

In the first book, "Saving Noelle," we learned of God's love for us. We discovered His willingness to chase us no matter how far we run. God never wants His children living in their darkest hour. His Word, The Bible, tells us that He is the lamp that will light our way. He doesn't want us to stumble and fall. However, if we do, He is there to pick us up and carry us if He must. Noelle ran, not knowing who He was. In her running, God made a way for her to find Him. You see He will never leave us out there by ourselves. Separation from God only happens by our choices not by His. Noelle's choice was to accept Him as her Lord and Savior. Through God, Noelle found salvation and eternal life.

God gave others the opportunity to receive their blessings when He opened the doors for them to help Noelle and they walked through. Angelina was willing to share the saddest time of her life. Through that willingness to be obedient, even when it hurt, Noelle was able to find her way to a loving Savior. By finding Him, she was able to make the right decisions when it came to the life of her baby. God opened his arms wide and Noelle came broken and spilled out willing to be captured by His love.

Through that process, God rewarded Angelina for her faithfulness to serve Him. The life that she saved became her own grandchild and Noelle became her new daughter. God's plans are always more than we could imagine. His abundance is above and beyond. There was no way for Angelina to know the direction that God was going to take her family. She walked in blind faith. She chose to serve a living God. She had prepared herself for an opportunity like the one that presented itself by serving on a daily basis. It was such a deep part of who she was that when God directed Noelle to her home, she was obedient without question.

Do you hold onto God daily? Are you practicing His ways so that when you are called you can answer? His ways are not our ways. Only by obediently following Him daily can we be sure that we do not miss the opportunities that He sends our way. Those opportunities may not look like anything that we could imagine. Just as the blessing, that we will receive will be more than we could comprehend.

As we moved into the second novel in the "CARRIED BY ANGELS SERIES", we see how God is masterminding Noelle's healing and giving her a future. The Lord gave us His promise in

Jeremiah 29:11
"For I know the plans I have for you," declares the LORD, "Plans to prosper you and not to harm you, plans to give you hope and a future. Then you will call upon me and come and pray to me, and I will listen to you. You will seek Me and find Me when you seek Me with all your heart. I will be found by you," declares the LORD, "and will bring you back from captivity.

It was Brad's plans to make sure that he was waiting on the Lord and because of his obedience, we watched as God gave him a future. God used Noelle, broken and desperate, to fulfill the desires of Brad's heart. God used Brad to open the door to an amazing new life in the Lord for Noelle and himself. After all, it would have been easy to ignore the call of God in the situation where Brad found himself. Yet, he chose to love in the perfect and flawless love of the Lord. There was no fear for Brad as he embraced the feelings that he had for Noelle. Why, because God's promise is, His love is perfect and perfect love drives out fear. He chose to have God as His shield and take refuge in Him. He let God arm him with strength and he stood on his **ROCK....JESUS CHRIST.**

I marvel at how God works. Let's look at the Prophet Elijah. He showed unconditional loyalty to the Lord and God took care of him. Elijah called forth a drought in the land to punish the nation for its idolatry. Yet God had him go to a place of peace where he could drink and God sent Ravens to feed him. Then when the brook dried up because of the drought, God sent him to a widow who was going to eat her last meal with her son and then die for lack of food. Elijah told her, under the direction of the Lord, to feed him first. She obeyed and made that last meal for Elijah and the Lord made her meals plenty. See how God used someone who was desperate to minister to Elijah. God gave the widow a chance to be obedient which then allowed God to bless the widow and her son. You can find this story in *I Kings 17:1-16.*

Brad and Angelina saw blessings because they were willing to be obedient and walk in the perfect love of the Lord. Noelle was blessed because she surrendered all to the Lord.

In the third book that is coming, **"FORGIVING FREEDOM"**, we are going to watch as the opportunity for forgiveness tears open healed wounds. Just like faith is a verb, so is forgiving. It requires an action that is not always comfortable. Will Brad and Noelle, with a bright new future looming ahead of them, be willing to walk into the darkness to see true freedom abound? We will see as **FORGIVING FREEDOM** broaches yet another principle near to God's heart... forgiveness.

As always, it has been my pleasure to open up another page in the life of the characters that we have come to love. I hope that as God writes their story for you, we will see them rise to the occasion created for them. My prayer will be that God's principles will live out on the pages of their books and that you will be able to find him in the midst of the words.

If this story has left you desperate to know the love of our God and you want to surrender your life to the God, I would love to pray with you right now. It does not matter where you are in your life, God will find you when you cry out to Him. Now is the time. It is never too early or too late. He is just waiting for you to come to Him. He will not push His way in. He wants it to be your choice to love Him. He gave you free will. He did not create you to be a robot. It has to be a choice that you make. He wants it to be your choice to love Him. He is a God of relationship and His relationship with you was important enough that He sent His son to die on the cross. If you are ready to receive love that knows no boundaries, you can just repeat this prayer after me:

Lord Jesus I come to You completely surrendered. I realize that I need a Savior. I confess that I am a sinner and that I need You. I want to be Your child and heir to Your eternal kingdom. I believe that You died on the cross for my sins. I believe that You were dead and buried and that on the third day You rose from the grave. Thank you for cleansing me from my sins, for removing them as far as the east is from the west. I am grateful that You see me white as snow. Thank you for making me a new. My old ways are gone and now I am a new creation bought and paid for by the precious blood of Jesus. I am now Your child and I will never be separated from You again. By praying this prayer I have sealed my place in Heaven forever to live with You. I acknowledge that I could never be worthy without You and that only by Your blood, and Your grace, and Your mercy can I be free. Thank you for forgiving me and for loving me as Your own. In Jesus name, Amen

Congratulation if you just prayed that prayer for the first time. On the other hand, maybe this was a recommitment because you had slipped away from your first love and wanted to rededicate you life back to the God who loves you. Do not feel guilt. He loves you wherever you find yourself in life. He is standing with arms opened wide to welcome you. Find a Bible. Begin to read His word. Fill up the God hole that only He can fill. He wants nothing but the best for you.

Do not let satan come in and steal from you anymore. He will try. He does not want you living in freedom. Satan's words are pain, suffering, destruction,"anger, bitterness, resentment, jealousy, all words that destroy your life. Close the door on your old life and open the door on your new life.

2 CORINTHIANS 5:17
Therefore, if anyone is in Christ,
He is a new creation; the old has gone,
the new has come.
2 Corinthians 5:20
We are therefore Christ's ambassadors,

213

as though God were making His appeal
through us. We implore you on Christ's behalf: Be reconciled to God.
God made Him who had no sin to be sin for
us,
So that in Him we might become the
righteous of God.

*For now, God bless you and yours and may
all of your dreams come true as you
encounter the Living Lord. God loves you.
Be captured.*

Brenda Conley
Angel Wing Ministries

Jeremiah 29:11
For I know the plans I have for you
These books continue to be an
obedience to serve God. It is still

my desire that whoever reads these words will find a burning passion to know my Savior more.

I would love to hear from you.

Like us on Facebook

Follow us on Twitter

Coming soon
www.angelwingministries.com

Watch for book three of the

Carried By Angels Series:

Forgiving Freedom

Coming soon!

Forgiving Freedom

Psalm 32
Blessed is he whose transgressions are forgiven,
whose sins are covered.

"Young man, this is a horrendous crime that you've been accused of committing. I don't feel like you're taking seriously the direction that your life just turned." Judge Owen Marshall was starring deeply into the eyes of, what he would classify as, 'the little rich boy' standing in front of him.

"Oh no sir…I understand fully what's happening here today. But…I didn't do it. Do you understand? I'm pleading not guilty." Delmyn Whitehall stood before the Judge in his three-piece suit, immaculate starched white shirt and classic tie. He stood with arrogance and pride wearing a smug look of someone who had it all together. He was confident and sure. His Dad was going to get all of this worked out. By the end of this arraignment, this nightmare was going to be nothing but a technicality. Any minute now, he would be free again and that would be none too soon for him. He'd had enough of all of the noise in that infernal place. Yesterday they had brought some riff raff into the cell and the person was just stupid. A whole day listening to him yelling about knowing his rights and wanting to talk to his lawyer had been enough for Del. The guy was strung out on something crazy and he didn't even know his name let alone his rights. Oh yah, he was ready to get out of this mess right now.

In any other location, it would have been difficult to determine between their roles. However, they were not in any other situation and the judge was not impressed with Delmyn's demeanor.

"Mr. Whitehall I understand more than you think. I understand that you are an obnoxious, arrogant punk who doesn't have enough sense to show respect to the person of authority who will play a part in making decisions that will affect your life forever." Judge Marshall continued. "Further more, you have an attorney representing you and I am silencing you. From this moment on, I will only hear from Mr. Mohan. Is that clear Mr. Mohan? Otherwise your client will be in contempt of court."

"Yes sir Your Honor." Teo Mohan respectfully answered while he grabbed a hold of his client's suit jacket and gave it a quick jerk. He hoped that Delmyn got the message to shut his mouth.

"Hey wait a minute. I pay for this attorney and I'll say when he talks or when he doesn't." Del opened his mouth again.

Mohan thought, obviously he did not understand my tug. "Your Honor…if I may have a moment with my client?"

Banging his gavel, Judge Marshall decreed, "That will be $100.00 fine with another night served in the jail for Mr. Delmyn Whitehall. Bailiff, remove this man from my court."

Del began to scream, "You can't do that. I'm not going to stay another night." Turning to face his Dad, Del pleaded, "Dad? Do something. He cannot talk to me like this. I am not going back there. I can't"

218

The Bailiff was already ushering him out of the courtroom. Murmurings built to a low roar rushing as a wind from the disbelief of the others in the room. They were excited to see the rich boy fall.

"Son, stop arguing. You're only making the situation worse," Del's dad, Keefe Whitehall, pleaded with his son. His heart was breaking. He did not understand how any of this was happening. His son was a good boy. He could never do any of the terrible things that those girls were saying. He understood that boys would be boys. He also understood that some girls put themselves in situations that could bring them trouble. The world was full of good girls and then there were…you know… the bad girls. What is Del to do when the bad girls throw themselves at him? After all, he is only human. His body anatomy responds differently. It is not his fault. Right? Besides what was he going to tell Shauna, Del's mother. She was back at their home waiting for her son to come back to the house with his dad. This was not going at all the way that he had hoped it would go. What good was the attorney he had hired? After paying out all of that money, Keefe had anticipated things would have gone differently."

"Dad…do something! I can't go back there." Del was yelling over his shoulder as the Bailiff closed the door.

"Next case. Anderson vs. the State of Georgia." The courtroom clerk announced.

"What?" Keefe looked at the attorney who was walking towards him. "What happened?" He asked.

Taking the arm of the father, Teo Mohan said, "Let's talk outside." And he walked him straight out of the courtroom doors and to a near by bench in a private alcove.

"Mr. Whitehall, what happened in there was a display of immaturity. Your son must learn to keep his mouth shut. No Judge is going to allow disrespect for his authority in his courtroom. On top of that, the felony that they have charged him with is a crime of total disrespect for another human life. We are going to have a hard time convincing a jury that your son respects others when the show that he puts on bears the resemblance of the total opposite. Now I suggest that if he calls you, it would be to his advantage for you to convince him that tomorrow when he appears before Judge Marshall again, he resembles a changed man. I expect that his demeanor would be apologetic and humble." Teo said.

"Humble?" Keefe questioned.

"Yes sir…humble. It is not a sign of weakness. It is a good character trait for any man to exhibit." Teo ended with a look on his face that said he was finished.

"Well maybe he needs a different attorney, if that's the best advice that you can give?" Keefe Whitehall rose up to his almost six-foot height.

"That is the best advice that I or any other attorney could give. Nevertheless, if you think that is not good enough for you and your son, then fine. If that is what you want, go for it. I promise you my heart will not break if I do not have to deal with your son's ill temper. He's the most arrogant, irresponsible young man that I've had the uncanny luck to meet in a long time." With that, Teo Mohan turned to leave.

Keefe, realizing what it would look like if his son walked back into the courtroom tomorrow with a different attorney said, "Wait…Mt. Mohan…let's not get hasty. After all, you have already spoken with my son. I think that we should continue as is, for the time being anyway. Do not get me wrong. I do understand that my son can be a bit, shall we say 'anxious' from time to time. Will you be seeing him before tomorrow?" He politely asked.

"It would not be my first choice. However, I will make it a point to see him and give him instruction before we enter that courtroom again. I may have been lax in assuming he would have understood the importance of showing the judge respect." Teo hoped that he had driven home his point that respect is something that Del should have learned at an early age from his parents.

"I would appreciate any help that you could give him. His mother is going to be so disappointed that he is still in jail. I'm not sure what I'm going to tell her."

"I suggest that you tell her the truth. Tell her that her son was belligerent to the judge and he got his hands slapped. Let her know that it is not going to go well for him if he does not learn some respect before we get into this. Maybe if he calls her she could talk some sense into him. With that, Teo turned to leave. Having second thoughts he turned back saying, "Mr. Whitehall, just so you can prepare your wife, this isn't going to be pretty. I have seen the girls' statements. The press is going to grab a hold of this. This will sell papers. You will find your son on every TV news show. There will be reporters digging into every aspect of Delmyn's life. Probably you and your wife will get drug through the eye of the needle also. Get ready. Your life is about to be tipped upside down. I suggest that you let your son know that too. We are in for a fight. It does not sound to me like these girls are going to back down. In fact there are more girls speaking up by the hour. This is beginning to appear to be a pattern. We are not dealing with a one time occurrence." Tipping his head to the broken father, he turned and walked away.

Standing in the hall alone in the crowd of people, Keefe questioned silently to a son who wasn't even there, *Del, what have you gotten us into this time?*

PROVERBS 16:3
Commit to the Lord
whatever you do;
And your plans will succeed.

God Bless

Notes

31099424R00158

Made in the USA
Middletown, DE
19 April 2016